Abducted

Sara Schoen

Abducted

Limitless Publishing, LLC
Kailua, HI 96734
www.limitlesspublishing.com

Formatting: Limitless Publishing

ISBN-13: 978-1-68058-016-7
ISBN-10: 1-68058-016-7

Dedication

I would like to dedicate this book entirely to the Wattpad community, my fans, friends and supporters that read Amber Alert, begged for more and encouraged me to keep writing. Without them I wouldn't have had the courage to publish, or to work harder on my favorite stories so they could one day be in print as well. They supported me, encouraged me, and they deserve all the thanks for helping me get my works out into the world, and outside of Wattpad alone. Many bought Amber Alert, and still encourage me to continue. I can't thank them enough, their unflappable support is the most amazing thing I've ever experienced. Thank you guys, I hope you enjoy this series again and again.

Prologue

"Well, Mr. Bennett, how does it feel?" the guard questioned as the metal food tray clanked on the metal bars, spewing some of the food onto the floor.

"How does what feel?" I asked, humoring him. He had come by every day with some crass humor to get a reaction out of me, but after twenty years he had failed—today would be no different.

"Knowing you're about to die."

It was getting down to days now, roughly ten, but it didn't affect me—all emotions had been beaten out of me in the first few weeks of my incarceration. I had been found guilty of kidnapping, murder, and rape; the other prisoners didn't take lightly to those charges.

The bodies of all my girls were found, including Kelly, because of Anna's determination to have me receive the death penalty or life in prison. Everyone would be pleased when I was dead. All of their precious children would be safe at last, but they didn't know what was really going to happen when I was dead.

I laughed slightly at the thought, "No different than it did yesterday when you asked."

"What about Anna not coming to visit you for your last days?"

That name struck a chord with me. Lovely Anna, my most beautiful wife yet, the one who took Kelly's betrayal off my mind and healed my heart for the first time in years. If Kelly hadn't turned, deciding she could no longer be with me, and attempted to escape, I never would have met Anna. Anna was so wonderful, perfect even, but then she fell in love with my bastard of a son. He ruined everything. I could have had Anna all to myself if I had just killed him when I had the chance—but Kelly would have left me for sure if I hadn't taken him for her.

Garrett was the perfect fit for her misery. After the loss of our child during birth, she needed a baby. She needed something to take care of. But when he grew up, she fought. I couldn't have that; I should have killed him while I was at it. Then Anna and I could be together still, the perfect marriage, both so happy in the relationship, willing to please the other and living peacefully.

"Anna will come," I said confidently, lifting the plastic spoon to my mouth.

"What, didn't anyone tell you?" he asked, with genuine pleasure in his tone that he would be the one to deliver the news. "She moved. Anna Cowles packed up and left. She's not coming to see you. By now, she's probably married Garrett and taken his last name, I can't tell you it, just in case, but it's so generic that she could be anyone. For all we know she could have changed her first name too. She isn't coming."

The spoon dropped out of my hand and fell on the plate. The guard laughed, finally getting that reaction he'd wanted. He left as another guard came to my cell escorting a visitor. This guard was polite, and even though he may not agree with my views, he always treated me with respect as well—as he did with all the prisoners.

"That is why you work to have the perfect family. They will never leave you, never betray you, and always listen," I said to the visitor the guard had escorted to my cell. "When Kelly attempted to leave, it drove me mad. We had the perfect relationship, and she was going to ruin it. Everyone was jealous of what we had, a high school sweetheart love that just never ended. Then when we lost the child, she couldn't even stand to look at me anymore."

The visitor was focused on me as I rushed to tell him everything. He had come multiple times in the last three years, but I had never instructed him on what to do until now. I needed to make sure he was dedicated, and that he would be willing to do anything.

"When she tried to leave, it shattered the world we had created together. We were happy; it wasn't forced on her. She chose to be with me, but when she chose to leave, I couldn't handle that. I locked her in the house with Garrett as a child, but when he grew up, she realized just how trapped she was and fought back. It should have taught me there shouldn't be other people allowed in the house—no one else until the person has fully accepted their fate. Kelly didn't, and when she chose to fight, she lost. I was devastated and took those girls in to fill the void, but they fought and couldn't be released."

I watched as his eyes gave away his emotions. He was torn, but he would do the job. It was only fair; he got what he wanted, and so did I.

"'The Chase' began by accident. Kelly escaped, and I tracked her down so I could keep her with me forever. It was enjoyable and thrilling. The fear of getting caught was exhilarating, although I never was. At least until Anna came along. She was too determined to escape, and she had too much to fight for. Then I made the mistake of bringing in another person to make her happy, the same mistake I'd made with Kelly. I thought she had accepted her fate, but it just gave her more incentive."

A soft sigh escaped my lips before I began speaking again. "Those girls were never meant to be found. They sealed my fate, and now I will be dead to join them in the afterlife. All I can say is that I hope you learn from my mistakes and make fewer of your own." There was a long pause between us, "And remember, never let anyone take your family away from you. By whatever means necessary, never let them take away your family!"

I watched as the man stood before me; he didn't say anything before he walked away. He was my apprentice, and my legacy.

Chapter 1

I glanced around. There wasn't any way to move in the crowded house without running into another person. The house was almost completely filled with people, and all the furniture had been moved to give extra space to the guests. At least this person thought ahead. The last house party I went to had the furniture out during the party and it was destroyed about an hour in. The whole night was filled with the cracking of wooden furniture and crashing of broken lamps and vases. The kid got busted; there is no way to make a good enough explanation for why the furniture is broken—no excuses are going to cover that up, especially when your parents walk in on you getting laid. He hadn't been to school the last few days; his parents must be having a field day with him for breaking the rules.

I squeezed through the large throng of people dancing. The music pounded in my ears as I walked past the sound system and into the kitchen. Bottles of alcohol covered the table and counters. There were different colors for fun-loving people, hard-core liquor for the experienced partiers and the 'start off liqueurs for first timers.

I thought about taking the starters so I could walk home when this was over, but when four stark-naked boys ran past me, I couldn't stop myself. My hand automatically reached toward the vodka—I definitely didn't want to remember that in the morning.

The liquid sloshed around in my cup with each unsteady step. I stopped walking and glanced over those who were too drunk to care they were basically having sex in the middle of the dance floor with their so called "dance moves".

"Wow." The sight disgusted me, but I was also slightly jealous. I wished that I had a hook-up to go to tonight, but I'm a one-man kind of girl.

As the cup touched my lips, I felt a hand grasp my butt, sending me forward slightly. The alcohol was starting to affect me, I guess.

I looked up to see Mark Troxley, standing over me with a similar red Solo cup in his hand. "Can I help you with something?" I asked, slightly rudely.

"Actually, I was hoping you'd say that," he said with a smile, as he took my cup from my hand and placed his and mine on the table behind him.

"Why is that?" I asked, a smile tugging at my lips.

"Would you like to dance?" he asked, pressing himself against me.

"Sure," I smiled, as I felt the reason he wanted to "dance" with me.

I ground my body against his, and he stood against the wall. His lips found mine while his hands traveled over the fabric of my dress. I licked his bottom lip to ask for entrance, and he accepted without hesitation. I lost my balance at the feeling of his tongue dancing against mine—my mind blurred, and my breathing picked up. His hands clasped onto my hips so that he could hold me closer to him and didn't move the whole time we were together.

I could hear his breathing start to match mine as he started to feel the intense emotion that had already strangled my heart. He began to pull me tighter to him in an attempt to get closer, which wasn't possible since there wasn't an inch of space between us—although I knew one way to get closer, and I needed it badly.

He must have needed it too, because he soon led me away from the party. We escaped upstairs to an empty room. He took off his shoes and left a sock on the door before locking it. The few moments were slightly blurred. I laid on the bed, and Mark slowly slid off my panties, dropping them to the floor as he raked his eyes over the prize he had won. I could hear the soft sigh escape his lips as he spoke, "God, you're beautiful, Audrey!"

I heard his zipper come undone, and glanced down to see the Lucky Brand classic saying 'lucky you' written on the zipper flap. I looked into his eyes. They were hungry, silently begging that I was okay with what we were about to do. I laid on my back and arched my hips to give him entrance in anticipation for what was coming. He didn't need to be told twice.

"Glad you're so eager. I know this will be good, my little rebel," he said with a soft sigh and a pleased smile tugging on the corners of his mouth.

***

I was so close to finishing; I gripped onto the headboard so I wouldn't hit my head while Mark started to pick up speed. The sounds of the party were drowned out by the noises of our moaning.

"God, you feel so good," he groaned, as he felt me spasm beneath him, the ball of pressure had finally burst into a sense of pure pleasure. Ever since my first time with him, I knew I would be his constant hook-up. He refused to date, since he wasn't yet of age, but whenever he needed a girl, I was his call. At first I was hurt that he wouldn't ask me out, but then I didn't care. It was because of the rules that he couldn't; I was sure on his birthday in a few days he would ask me to be his girlfriend.

Well, he might. I couldn't be sure, though, since it was actually illegal to date until we were eighteen. While I was eighteen, I was waiting for Mark's birthday; then we could be official. It was another stupid law that was made after Anna Cowles was kidnapped; I couldn't believe half of them even passed. Of course, parents were in such a state of fear they would have voted for anything to protect their children. Too bad for them, they didn't realize that the laws would just make it more fun for teenagers to break the rules.

We hated the rules; they were stupid, ignorant, and provided no protection. Most times we just broke the laws, but sometimes, we'd get caught and then that meant trouble. Just as Mark finished fixing his jeans, there was a bang on the door that caused both of us to jump.

"Don't people know what it means when the door is locked and there's a sock on the door?" Mark asked with a chuckle as he toyed with my underwear with a mischievous smile. "Be sure to find me again in three days. I have something I want to ask you then."

I felt a wide smile spread across my face. He was going to ask me to date him, I just knew it. I was about to answer when the door was kicked in and slammed into the wall. Two police officers came into the room to see Mark with my underwear in his hand and my appearance disheveled.

"I would like to see you talk your way out of this one, Audrey. Anna and Garrett will not be pleased," a family friend, Officer James Sparks, said, as Mark and I raced out of the room. But Officer Sparks caught me, and allowed me to fix my appearance before he grabbed my arm roughly and led me from the house. Arrested for breaking three laws at once: breaking curfew, underage alcohol consumption, and resisting arrest for being in a locked room and trying to run. Maybe if I was lucky they couldn't get me on breaking the relations law.

How was I going to explain this one to mom and dad?

Chapter 2

Houses flew by as James sped toward my house to take me home. The party broke up when I was arrested for the third time this year. The first time was the new curfew law. A few days after it was established, I was out twenty minutes after curfew because Mark and I had been together, and I was arrested while walking home. The second time was for breaking the supervision law, which stated everyone under the age of eighteen was to be watched by an adult at all times, unless written permission was granted. I had ditched school. A teacher noticed and had to report it to the police in case another kidnapping had occurred. They picked me up from a McDonald's and arrested me for it; it was almost as serious as a bomb scare to them now.

I couldn't believe it when the laws passed, and I can't believe that they were actually enforced. Who's going to keep track of how old I am so I don't need written permission to leave an adult's line of sight? Why does it matter if I choose to date before I'm of age, anyway? The rules were meaningless, they did nothing to help our safety—

they made us weaker, in my opinion—and only officers and parents cared about them. Everyone ate it up. Too bad parents didn't know that their rules would make a generation of total rebels and sneaky kids.

"I can't believe I'm the one who has to tell your parents this," James said, as he pulled me out of the car so I wouldn't try to run again.

I swallowed nervously as James knocked on the front door of my house. I could just imagine what my parents were going to say when they saw the flashing police lights. James bringing me home yet again—only this time would be worse, because he caught me with my legs spread waiting for Mark to give in to my primal needs.

I cringed as the door opened, and I saw my mother wrapped in my father's arms. Their faces were sullen with disappointment, and I could see the tears in my mom's eyes. It made me feel bad, but I didn't regret what I did. I actually wished that I could do it again, but this time get dressed before James broke the door down. Maybe then I could have faked that the door had just locked behind us, or at least jumped out of the bedroom window to escape.

"What did she do now, James?" Garrett asked, as he attempted to sooth my mother's tears.

"She was found on a bed with her dress pulled up her around her waist, a young man holding her underwear, but she was arrested for breaking three laws at once. Underage drinking, breaking curfew, and resisting arrest—for a while there she tried to run away," James said, as he pushed me lightly into the house. "If we catch her again, she goes to jail. I'm sorry, Anna, Garrett. I wish I could come over on better circumstances," James finished. He turned around and walked back to his car.

"Come inside, Audrey," I heard my father say, as he held the door open for me.

I actually contemplated running, but I knew that wouldn't work. I would eventually have to come back home, so I took a deep breath and walked inside. My mother was already sitting at the kitchen table with my six-year-old sister, Kate. I sighed, knowing exactly the direction this discussion was going to take. Maybe I should run, then I could avoid this conversation for just a little longer, but I could feel my father's presence close behind me. Running was no longer an option.

"Audrey, what were you thinking?" I heard dad ask as I pulled out a seat and sat down at the table.

"I wasn't," I stated, knowing that if I played along this would go by faster, and I could hide in my room so I could wallow in embarrassment. Arrested three times, police walking in on us after the act, Mark wouldn't even think of dating me now, and his birthday was three days away. I was so close!

"You're just telling me what I want to hear," my father said smartly.

"You're right," I said with a sigh.

"You're eighteen now, Audrey. I thought this would stop once you turned eighteen; you're above some of these laws now. You're no longer affected by most of them, that's probably why it was only three offenses this time, but it's gotten worse!" he said. He raked his fingers through his short hair, but his hair just snapped right back into place as if it had never been disturbed.

"Then why was I arrested?" I asked stupidly—I needed to learn to think before I spoke.

"You mean besides breaking curfew, which you can't do until you're in college, where they have their own rules, underage drinking, and resisting arrest? James caught you about ready to have sex with someone. Do you even know the meaning behind that?"

"Yes, it's a beautiful thing, and it's between two people who love each other. Wasn't mom like this when she was younger?" I asked turning to my mother, all the color quickly drained from her face. Her face was blank, but she on the verge of tears. I must have really upset her this time.

"Your mom's childhood was different than others', Audrey."

"Why?" I asked. My mom seemed to be fighting to hold down her dinner.

"That's not important right now. Right now, we have to worry about your behavior. You're supposed to be setting an example for Kate, but instead you're acting like a common criminal. You need to straighten up, and no more seeing this kid that was ready to take advantage of you while you were drunk," my father said as he got up to take Kate back to bed.

"I've been seeing him for over a year! You can't just tell me to stop!"

"You've been what? That's illegal, Audrey if he's younger than you!" Dad spat at me.

"It wouldn't be if Anna Cowles hadn't been so stupid to get herself kidnapped!" I yelled back at him. "She's the reason these rules even exist!"

"It wasn't just Anna, Audrey!" My mother said forcing herself from her chair. At least now she had color returning to her face, too bad for me that color was red from anger. "There were twelve other girls before her that were taken! She's the only one that escaped and made it out alive."

"If she had died-" I started, but my mother quickly interrupted me.

"Then another girl would have gone through what she did, and maybe even a few more after that! Eventually he would have been found, and these rules may still be in effect. These regulations were made to protect you, and whether you like them or not they are here to stay! Now go to bed—I don't want to see you for the rest of the night!" my mother yelled, shouting at me for the first time in my life. I knew I had disappointed her, and it crushed my heart, but I didn't regret the choice.

"Fine," I said sourly, as I briskly walked out of the room and upstairs to my bedroom.

I didn't look back when my father tried calling me back downstairs. I didn't want to hear what he had to say. He would take my mom's side like always, even if she was wrong.

They had showed me just how much love can mean in a person's life while growing up, because they always stood together. They had been together for almost twenty years, and their love had never died. I had watched them every day when I was little, just praying I would find someone who cared for me like they cared for each other. They were both so overly cautious, though; I'm amazed they even decided to date each other by how guarded they were.

Their childhood must have sucked, but I wouldn't know since they didn't talk about it. I couldn't get my grandparents to tell me about them as children. It was as if their childhood years, my father from the age of ten until he was nineteen, and my mother from sixteen to twenty, was a total blank. I couldn't find pictures or get anyone to talk about them; it was like it never happened, but everyone would tell me how happy they were together. It was easy enough to see just by the smiles on their faces and the sparkle in their eyes when they talked about each other. They truly loved each other, but I didn't think that love was passed onto me. They hated that I didn't follow the rules; they were too over protective and overbearing when it came to me.

What had I done wrong? Nothing. So why were they punishing me by preventing me from being with friends and having a boyfriend like a normal teenager? It wasn't my fault. It wasn't any of our faults; it was Anna Cowles' fault, but my mom was right. If Anna hadn't been the one to escape, then someone else would have been taken, and eventually one of them might have escaped. The rules would have been made either way, one day, or Steve Bennett would still be out there. That thought sent a shiver down my spine.

I realized how wrong I was. I was acting out against the laws because they were unfair to teens, but it wasn't Anna's fault. She was just the push for it that people used so the laws could pass. She was a front, not the reason.

"Fine, I'll just apologize, and everything will be okay again. Then I can go back to hating these stupid laws and Anna Cowles," I said to myself as I forced myself out of bed.

I glanced at Kate's closed bedroom door and sighed. I did need to be a better example, but once she grew up she would realize why I was acting like this and probably react the same way. The laws were unfair, overbearing, and insane! They didn't make any sense as to how they would protect me. Most didn't seem to connect to the string of kidnappings, they were just another excuse to box teens in. They should have known that strict laws make for sneaky kids.

I was careful to avoid any of the squeaking stairs as I made my way back downstairs, just in case they had fallen asleep after they took Kate to bed. I lightly curled my toes into the carpet and let a small smile tug on the corners of my lips. I loved the carpet, it was warm and soft, unlike the tile or hardwood flooring that covered my friends' houses. My mother was always adamant about not having hardwood floors, I'm not sure why, but at this moment I didn't care. The carpet was welcoming as I took a deep breath to gather my courage.

I was about to step out to see my parents when I heard my father talking. "We can't tell her what happened. It won't change her mind about the laws, and it will only change her perspective on us. Anna Cowles has been the fall guy for years, and used to push for these laws. Even our daughter blames her for the laws that others claimed would help, but they haven't. These laws don't make any sense, but if we tell her that, she will think it's okay to keep getting arrested. She will continue to put herself in danger, and that will cause something bad to happen."

"I didn't support those laws though, Garrett," my mother responded. There was an edge in her voice that made me cringe, she was about to cry again.

"I know you didn't, but your recovery was the push point. My name doesn't come up nearly as much because of how long I was gone. You were the one that told the story, so subsequently, you are the one that is well known for it."

"You should have told it," my mom said with a sad sigh.

"I was only a witness, you were the main individual that was needed to put Steve behind bars."

I poked my head around the corner to see him holding my mother. The mention of the Steve Bennett case increased my curiosity. They were talking as if they had been there for it, but they had always told me they didn't live in Virginia, and they didn't know Anna Cowles either.

"I'm glad you were there through it all. I couldn't have done it without you. I love you, Garrett."

"I love you too, Anna, but I think you could have done it if I hadn't made it through the beating. You were stronger from the experience, and while my loss would have hurt, you could have done it."

"Maybe, but then no one would come within ten

feet of me. No one would want to date me after being kidnapped and defiled," my mom said with a light laugh in her voice.

"They wouldn't know what they were missing then, because you're an amazing person and an even better wife. Even if you wouldn't let me name one of our daughters Kelly," Dad said with a laugh as my mom slapped him on the back of the head.

"That's not funny," Mom stated with a giggle.

"It made you laugh, so I think it's funny."

"You always made me laugh, even when I was trapped in that house and we were screaming down each other's throats."

They laughed about old memories as I started to connect the dots. Did she say she was kidnapped and trapped in a house? My father had said she was the main witness. She said that she didn't advocate for these laws. I shook my head trying to get rid of the thoughts that my mom was Anna Cowles. My mom's name was Anna Williams until she married my father, then it became Anna Thomas—unless she changed it so she could move out of the area undetected. Why else would she have been the reason Steve was put behind bars? Could my mom be *the* Anna Cowles?

"Are you Anna Cowles?" I asked, emerging from behind my hiding spot.

"Audrey, we thought you were in bed," my mom said, avoiding my question.

"Are you Anna Cowles?" I asked, repeating my question.

"Audrey, we didn't want you to know because it would affect how you saw us. We wanted you to

18

have a normal childhood, one that we didn't have. In this case ignorance was for the best," my father said, taking over the conversation.

"You lied to me?"

"We did it in your best interest! Did you want to know that Steve Bennett took your mother from a public park in broad daylight and shot two people? Did you want to know she was tortured and there was nothing anyone could do about it? What good would that have done you?"

"I'm the child of *the* Anna Cowles! The girl that was forced into a psychopath's home because she didn't fight?" I blurted out in anger and betrayal.

"Audrey!" my mother shrieked.

"I hate you, and I never want to see either of you again!" I screamed as I ran out of the house. I heard their calls behind me, but by the time I was down the block I knew I was free. I had nowhere to go for the night, though; it was against the law to go over to friends' houses this late. Their parents would call the police on me, and I'd be taken right back home—but if I'm going to break another law tonight, it's going to be wiping my memory with alcohol.

I cut through yards and made my way downtown where Mark took me to get my first drink. They didn't check identification, and I was able to get a few drinks pretty easily. I didn't think about getting home afterward, I figured I would make a new friend while I was out anyway. I might as well get tipsy so I could flirt my way home.

"Give me one," I said to the bartender. He slid a beer my way, and I grimaced. I hated the taste, but it was all he would dish out to underage kids. It was against the law, but he got paid by every teen that came here and probably made more money like that. I gulped down the beer, knowing it would take a few more, but eventually I lost count of how many I had had. By that time the bartender had told me he thought I had enough and I was caught off.

"Do you want me to get you a ride home?" the bartender asked.

"I got her. I'm sure she won't mind," a deep voice said from behind me. I swiveled my chair and turned to see a handsome man in his early twenties with jet-black hair and light tanned skin. His smile was breathtaking, along with his enticing scent of fresh rain and flowers. It brought a smile to my lips.

"I wouldn't mind at all. I'm Audrey Thomas," I said, as I almost tipped out of my seat.

"I'm Damien Clark. Now let's get you home before you pass out," he said with a light chuckle that made me swoon. Or maybe that was the over-consumption of alcohol.

He wrapped his arms around me as he assisted me to the ground so we could walk out together. I ended up mostly leaning on him before he put me in his car and drove off. I watched as the streetlights faded away and were quickly replaced by trees. I didn't notice I wasn't going home until it was too late. He didn't even ask for my address—instead, I was going somewhere much more sinister, and I could only hope I would make it out alive.

Chapter 3

Sunlight hit me in the face. I moved to get away from the light, and my arm hit something solid. I shot up to see that my arm had hit Damien's bare chest. At first I was confused. How had I gotten here, and why I was with him? Then I remembered the bar, the drinking, and the amazing sex we had last night. He had been masterful and was pleasing to both my body and eyes.

So much for being a one man kind of girl; I was sure Mark wouldn't have asked me out after last night anyway. Too much happened. It was overwhelming, and Damien had been there when I needed an outlet.

As I looked at him, I could still feel the need to mold my body to his and feel his lips on my skin. He looked so peaceful sleeping, so mouth-wateringly handsome and seductive as when I met him in the bar. A small moan escaped my lips as I pictured him over me again. His eyes focused only on me as if I was the most important thing in the world.

"Careful, if you keep thinking about it I won't be

able to restrain myself," he said in a hazy voice.

His eyes fluttered open to reveal the stunning icy blue that had captivated me. Damien rolled over and wrapped his arms around my small frame to pull me toward him. I felt his lips trace the shape of my jawline as he pulled me on top of him. His naked form pressed against mine as he hugged me tightly.

"Good morning, beautiful," he growled seductively in my ear.

"Hey yourself, handsome."

Damien moaned slightly as a smile spread across his face. He tangled his fingers in my hair to pull my face to his again. His lips found mine easily, and in a few seconds the kiss turned heated before he pulled away.

"You are just so lovely. It's such a pity that I have to take you home," Damien growled, tracing his fingers down the curves of my body.

"I don't want to go home."

"Why not? What would send such a beautiful young lady running to a bar for comfort?"

"My parents spent eighteen years lying to me about who they are?"

"What do you mean?" Damien asked, as he kissed down the length of my neck.

"My mother is Anna Cowles, and my father is Garrett Thomas," I spat, as Damien continued to kiss a trail up my neck. He paused for a moment, the names must have shocked him—they were well-known.

"I'm sure they just wanted to keep you safe."

"I don't care. I don't want to go back. It's her fault the laws are like this; she was too stupid to take care of herself."

"Well then, what do you want to do, Audrey? We are kind of close to your home, and I have to take a trip today. I can't just leave you here to fend for yourself. What if someone came along to kidnap you?"

"I could defend myself," I stated proudly.

"Not all of the people that mean you harm make it so obvious," Damien said, before he kissed my lips.

"Well, were are you going for your trip?"

"I have to visit a family friend's home. He is away for a while, and I have to make sure his house is in order for his return."

"Could I come?"

"You want to come? Don't you have school today?" Damien teased, as a smirk curved his lips.

"I do, but I can skip."

"You're worried your parents will show up to talk to you, aren't you?"

"Yes," I stated honestly, as he toyed with my hair. I watched as he closed his eyes to think it over. He relaxed, showing off a square face and strong jaw—he truly was such a handsome man.

"I would love for you to come with me, Audrey. Just let me get ready, and we'll be on our way." I watched him pull on a pair of jeans and a blue plaid, button-up shirt. His icy blue eyes were watching me in the mirror the entire time.

"Would you like to shower? I don't know when we will be back, but the water there is shut off, and you may not be able to shower for a while."

"Yeah, I'll do that."

"I'll put your clothes in the wash so you have something clean to wear," Damien answered as he left the room, giving me one last kiss on his way out the door.

I smiled as I walked into the shower and rinsed off. The shampoo foamed in my hands as I scrubbed away the conversation with my parents last night. The water wrapped me in a protective covering, as I tried to understand their choice to lie to me. I watched the suds slowly run down the drain as I decided I needed more time away from them to think about it.

I hadn't realized how long I had spent in the shower until Damien knocked on the door. "You're clothes are dried. Whenever you're ready, breakfast is downstairs," he said, as he laid the clothes on the sink and closed the door behind him.

I shut off the water as my reply and stepped out of the shower. I quickly dried off and pulled on the skinny jeans over my damp legs. They snagged in a few places due to the moisture, but eventually got into place. The t-shirt pulled over easily and I was out the door before Damien could come to knock again.

I raced down the stairs and started eating quickly so he wouldn't leave without me. If he did, I would either get arrested or have to go to school, but both would take me straight to my parents.

"You know you'll have to see your parents again one day, right?"

"I will hold off on that for as long as I can," I stated, as I thought about how they must have felt waking up this morning and seeing me gone. They had probably called James, and he would be out searching for me. I needed to get out of town for a while. I could do that, I was old enough to take care of myself. I just needed Damien to get me out of town, and then I could come back when I was ready.

"You eat, and I will pack up the car."

"Is it a long trip?"

"It's about an hour. It's not far, but I still have to put some stuff in the car. Just eat, and I will be ready in a few minutes," Damien said as he kissed my cheek.

I sat silently and thought over what had happened with my parents. I felt bad for yelling at them and saying I hated them. I didn't mean it; I was angry. They would understand when I got home. Every time we fought I ran out and left for a few days, then I was punished and it went back to normal. I'd go home after this trip with Damien—something fun before I get grounded again.

"You ready, Audrey?" Damien called, as I swallowed the last bite of waffle.

"Yeah, coming!"

"I was wondering what was taking you so long," Damien said, as he pulled me closer to him.

"Sorry to keep you waiting."

"You're worth the wait. Let's go." He ushered me to the door and slammed shut behind me.

The car ride was filled with chatter and laughter. I was getting to know Damien as a person, and he sounded remarkable. He had just finished school, was easy to talk to, and he captivated me with every word. We shared similar interests and thoughts; it was almost as if we had grown up together. He was so charming, in fact, that I hadn't noticed the car ride was longer than he had said it would be. I realized something was wrong when the car finally came to a stop on the gravel road. At first I was upset because I would have to get out and Damien would be busy, but as I glanced up at the house, fear took over my body. The windows were boarded up; there was no way any light could enter the house. The paint was chipping away, and it looked run down. The front door was shut, but I could see marks all over as if someone had forced their way in. Damien opened my door and took my hand.

"Damien, what are we doing here?"

"This is my friend's house. I'm here to house sit for him while he is gone. We already covered this, Audrey."

"This house looks like it was deserted, whose house is this?" I asked nervously.

"Steve Bennett's. We will be staying here for a while."

His words sent fear through my veins. Steve Bennett, the man who kidnapped twelve girls, including my mom, was due for death by lethal injection in a few days. The feed from the old trial had been replaying on the television for months; Anna Cowles' interview was replayed along with Steve's. There were new analyses of Steve's interviews and speech patterns every time the television was turned on.

Without thinking, I turned around and started running toward the road to go home, but Damien grabbed my waist and pulled me back before I could get far.

"You're not going anywhere, Audrey. If you ever make it out of this alive, you and your mother will finally have something in common: a fear of this house." He lifted me over his shoulder and carried me inside.

I squirmed and tried to fight against him, but once the door slammed shut, I knew I wasn't going to escape anytime soon.

Chapter 4

The front door was solidly in its place; it didn't want to open at all. In fact, Damien had to slam his body against the wooden blockade and force it open. There was only hardwood flooring, and it seemed I could hear every step we took echo through the house. It was bare to the bones; the walls held no photos or phones, and rooms remained empty of furniture unless it was bolted to the ground.

"Damien, what are you doing?" I cried, as he forced me into a hard wooden chair. I felt rope secured to my arms and legs as Damien turned away from me. He left the room, leaving the fear to take over my body as I struggled to free myself. I could hear his footsteps as they traveled upstairs and moved over my head. The steady footfalls brought a new sense of fear as he re-entered the room.

"I'm doing what I was told to do," he said with a shrug, as he produced a camera that I hadn't seen since I was a child. "Say cheese." The Polaroid clicked and slid out a photo, which Damien shook

Abducted

to help develop it.

"I meant why, you jerk!"

"Now, now, Audrey. No need to become rude."

"Why are you doing this to me?"

"I didn't originally plan it like this, if that helps you in any way."

"It doesn't," I spat.

"I didn't know you were Anna Cowles' daughter. Honestly, you were just a pretty girl that I wanted to get to know. You were so beautiful that I had to try, and maybe you could tell me something about Anna. You see, I didn't know where she was. It was my mission to take her daughter so that I could bring her out, but I couldn't do that because she changed her name and moved."

"Why do you need me?" I asked. My mother had been kidnapped and dragged here; it was almost poetic justice that I'm now stuck in the same house she was.

"Let me finish. Steve Bennett doesn't want to die, and what better way to keep him alive than to take someone that follows his profile—copycat parse. They'll have to let him out so he can help them find you."

"Why would you help him?"

"I have no choice..." Damien mumbled, as he walked out of the room and left me tied to the chair.

"Why not?"

"That's none of your business," Damien snapped.

"You have me here against my will! I think it's my business."

"See, that's where you're wrong. Here, you don't

think. You follow thirteen simple rules and do nothing outside of them."

"What rules?"

"The same ones your mother followed so expertly, until her betrayal was exposed. There were twelve at the time, except when she was thrown out of the house, Steve made another one." Damien slipped the piece of paper from the table and held it to my face.

1. Do as you're told.
2. Have all meals ready for me when I get home.
3. Make sure the house stays clean.
4. Never speak out of turn or back talk.
5. Do not argue. I'm right, you're wrong.
6. You belong to me and only me.
7. You take care of the house, I provide for the family.
8. You do not leave the house unless told so.
9. You treat me like a loving husband; I will be one.
10. Take care of the kid; he follows similar rules.
11. Never tell me no! See rule 1.
12. Do not try to hurt me. I over power you.
13. Don't lie or fake. I don't care if you don't like it here, because you're mine now.

If any of these rules are broken, punishment will ensue.

"Obviously, Garrett is no longer with us, so rule ten is no longer in effect. I will think of a different one to take its spot later," Damien said with a suggestive smile.

"Garrett?" I questioned skeptically.

"Yes, your father. Let me guess, they never told you how they met. What a pity. I hear it was a fantastic love story," Damien sneered.

"They met in college, he spilled coffee on her dress accidentally," I asserted, remembering what my parent's had told me when I asked. Damien just laughed, and had to lean against the wall for support when he couldn't stop.

"You actually believe that?" he questioned with a chuckle. "Well, I give them credit, they worked hard to cover up the past."

"What do you mean?"

"You honestly think that they met under normal circumstances, as if it was fate? If you do, you're stupid—everyone knows that they met in this house."

"I am not stupid!" I yelled back, as his hand landed on my shoulder. I didn't feel afraid, but I pulled my shoulder from his touch as he undid the bounds around my wrists.

"You were senseless with the information you gave me, a total stranger. So that makes you reckless, irresponsible, and stupid. You could have saved yourself from this," Damien spat, as he grabbed my wrist and dragged me through the bare halls of the house. I could hear the echoing clap of my footsteps as I was forced to follow Damien up the stairs. The second floor had a main room, with a large window, and then three smaller rooms connected to it. The large window was boarded up; I would never see daylight again.

"It's a pity you had to be Anna Cowles' daughter," Damien sighed, as he forced open one of the doors.

"Why?"

"Because I honestly liked you. I enjoyed the intelligent conversation and the lively company, but now I have to keep you trapped against your will. That will put quite the damper on our relationship."

"There is no relationship!" I spat, as he leaned closer to me.

"Don't say that, Audrey. I was thinking of changing rule number nine to treating me as the perfect boyfriend, and then rule ten would be to act as if you loved me."

"Wouldn't that cancel out rule thirteen then? I'd be faking!"

"I saw how you were last night. You won't be faking," Damien said with a laugh as he shut the door, leaving me alone and isolated.

The room was stripped to the bare necessities. There were no windows or wallpaper, just concrete walls, hard wooden floors, and a bed. The only wall decorations were thirteen pictures that hung on the wall. The girls didn't look familiar to me until I got to the one right before mine, my mother. I had seen photos of her from my grandmother's photo album, but none of them looked like this. I shivered as I stared at my mother's picture. It must have been horrifying living here, and now I was trapped like she had been.

My parents had warned me of the dangers of the world, the laws had tried to protect me, and the kidnappings were a typical conversation, but I still didn't listen. Now I was going to understand exactly what the laws had been trying to protect me from. I was going to have to live through what my mother did, and hopefully survive like she did.

Chapter 5

I tried to think of everything I knew about Steve Bennett to help me find a way out. His life had become a topic of study across the nation after he successfully captured thirteen girls. But since the laws had prevented us from learning details, and tried to save us from having another mass kidnapping, I didn't know as much as I should. My mom would know more, and my father would know even better. I needed to know about Steve so that I could find out how Damien was going to act. How was he going to treat me, and how was life in this house going to be?

I glanced at the photos again; my mother was the reason I was here, Damien had said so, and he had brought me here to drag my mother out of hiding.

Steve captured the girls to be a replacement wife for the one he lost, Kelly, which was common knowledge due to his ravings in jail. Damien didn't seem to want that since he didn't call me Kelly or try to make a move on me. I made all the moves on him, and look where that got me—trapped in a concrete room. I wish I had known sooner that my mom was Anna Cowles; I would appreciate it right now. I would know how she escaped and maybe what to expect; but if she had told me, I either wouldn't have believed her, or I would have run out on her as I just did.

I sighed in frustration. I wish that her photo could talk to me, tell me what she experienced and tell me how to get out. I just wanted to know what to expect, but Steve would be different than Damien.

I glanced at the photos again, and wondered how Damien was connected in all of this. What did Damien have to gain from taking me? He should know that people would start looking for me when I didn't go back home right away. The laws made it mandatory to report someone that hadn't been seen for a week. So what was worth the risk?

"Audrey, are you in there?" Damien's voice asked through the door.

"Well, it's not like I could go anywhere else," I retorted with a drawn out sigh.

"It was only out of courtesy; don't be rude," he said, as he walked in and handed me a black sweatshirt.

"What's this for?"

"It's going to get cold in the next few weeks. I don't want you to get sick," he said nonchalantly, as he turned and walked out of the room.

"I won't be here then." He stopped in his tracks as soon as the words left my mouth. I could see the anger in his eyes as he turned to glare at me.

"What's that supposed to mean?"

"I'll get out of here. My family will be looking

for me."

"I don't think they'll start looking for you for a while. You ran off, remember? Who's going to look for a runaway?"

"They will!"

"No, they won't. You screamed at them, told them you hated them, and said you wouldn't come back. You're not going anywhere."

He was right; no one was going to look for a runaway. I had run off a few times before, but I always came back. They would just wait for me to cool off and come back home, but I wasn't going to. I was going to be stuck here with no help, only myself. It wasn't a terrible thought; I have relied on myself since those laws took away my freedom, and I had to make my own.

"That's what I thought," Damien said as he turned to leave.

"I'll escape," I said, loud enough for him to hear me.

"I wouldn't try that, Audrey. This house holds a lot of secrets, and even more traps. You won't be getting out anytime soon, just accept it. You're going to live in this room for a long time," he said as he slammed the door behind him, not caring about what I said after he left.

"Fine, if I can't escape, I'm going to figure out what you want from me and why you're helping Steve. There's got to be something in this house," I said to myself.

I waited until I was sure Damien had gone down the stairs. I knew there were a few other rooms, one of which my father had stayed in while he and my mother had been trapped here together. My footsteps echoed off the hardwood floor as I traveled to the first room. It was an empty closet with nothing except a single hanger in it. I sighed heavily, then shut the door before moving on. I tried hard to keep my movements quiet, but the closet door squeaked, and I thought Damien would come sprinting up the stairs.

I took a relaxing breath as I made it to the next door, but it squeaked loudly—I froze. When I didn't hear Damien coming up the stairs, I slid into the room and turned on the light; I had found a bathroom. I glanced around and noted the necessities were there—toilet paper and towels—but my eyes fell on a brown paper bag. The bag crumpled as my hand wrapped around to pull it out. I cringed at how loud the paper bag was. I quickly dumped out the contents and threw away the bag; I figured the less time I held it the less noise I would make. In my hand, I held a leather-bound book that was smooth to the touch. I felt a smile turning up at the corners of my lips as I opened the book.

Inside there was a signature on the first page. It was signed by Garrett Thomas and titled *The Chronicle of a Survivor*. I laughed slightly as the door behind me creaked open.

"What do you think you are doing?" I heard Damien ask from behind me.

"Going to the bathroom," I said, hiding the journal behind my back—slowly placing it up my shirt to hide it from view.

"Let me see your hands," he ordered. I showed him my hands, but when he tried to turn me around

I had to think of a way to stop him. Without thinking, I stood up on my toes and kissed him lightly on the lips before turning and running away from him like a shy schoolgirl.

"Right," Damien said in drawn out disbelief, as I ran back to my room.

I knew kissing him was a cheap trick because it would distract him, but I needed to get out with the book. I had a strong feeling that my father had left me everything I needed to survive in this house. I could only hope I would finally listen to his advice so I could find my way back home.

Chapter 6

"So where are the other girls?" I asked Damien when I came out of my room for breakfast a few days later. He had left me alone for a while so that I could adjust, as he put it. I spent all that time reading my father's journal. I was thankful; even though his life was hell in this house, he took detailed notes so he could one day escape.

"What other girls?" he asked.

"You said you were a copycat, so there has to be other girls."

"I'm not an actual copycat. My job is just to make them think that they caught the wrong man. I need to get him out of jail somehow. Either they caught the wrong man, or they need his help to track me down."

"How does taking me help with that?"

"If Steve Bennett is in jail, how could he take you? If they couldn't find him the first time, then they will need help to prevent another mass kidnapping."

"So you only have to take one person to make the plan work?"

"Yeah, and why would I want another girl? I wouldn't want you to get jealous of other girls," Damien said with a wink as brought breakfast to me.

"How can I be jealous if you held us against our will?"

"It's common knowledge that Steve Bennett made love to his wives."

"You mean he raped them," I spat sourly. "Is that a threat Damien?"

"I would never threaten you. When we make love you'll want it, too. You'll just have to accept our relationship."

"There is no relationship."

"That's not what you were hoping for last night."

"I'm in a relationship with someone already. You were a one night thing," I said with a smirk, knowing that would irritate him.

"Must be a very open relationship for you to have sex with me while you were with them," he stated through gritted teeth.

"Well, it has to be open. It's illegal for individuals under eighteen to date, remember?"

"Nice way to avoid saying 'kids,' but you're old enough to date."

"But Mark isn't yet," I stated. Damien's face grew tense and irritated. He looked as if he was ready to punch something or someone; I just hoped I wasn't the target.

"Well, I guess now I don't have competition," Damien said with a smirk as his expression changed. He let out a soft chuckle before taking a seat next to me.

"What do you mean?"

"In a few days he'll forget about you. You were a hook-up; he'll find someone else."

"No he won't! He wants to date me," I asserted.

"Did he tell you that? In those words exactly?"

"No, but—"

"There are no buts in this case, Audrey. If he wanted to date you, he would have told you. Hell, if I was under eighteen, I'd tell you I wanted to date you."

"Too bad you're, what, thirty-five?" I said, letting the sarcasm drip from my words.

"I'm twenty-one, thank you very much. I'm actually allowed to drink and go to bars like where I picked you up. I can't believe the bartender even served you a drink. You are obviously underage," Damien spat in my face, as if it was an insult.

"Clearly not underage enough for you to take hostage."

"You came with me willingly. You should be thankful!"

"How can I be thankful?"

"You're the one that wanted a way out. You didn't want to go back."

"I didn't want to be trapped here either!" I retorted, as a frown creased onto his lips.

"Well, now you have no choice," he said, forcibly getting up from the table, causing the chair to fall roughly onto the floor.

"Where are you going?" I asked, as he reached for a jacket.

"I'm going to get food and clear my head before I try to find Mark and punch him," Damien stated through gritted teeth, as he fought with the door and finally forced it open.

The door slammed shut, the sound reverberated through the house, and left me standing in shock. It took me a few moments to realize that the car had driven off, and I was standing alone in the house. I tried to open the door, but I either wasn't strong enough to pull it open, or he had locked it from the outside. I walked through the bottom floor, but there wasn't a loose spot to take the boards off the windows. I was about to give up until my hand hit a hollow spot on the wall in the kitchen. My fingers slipped into one of the edges of the board. There was a small click that echoed through the empty house as I pried the door open. With all the strength I had in me, I was able to move the hidden door far enough for me to squeeze through.

There were a set of stairs that took me into a basement, but I wasn't sure why it was placed out of sight. The walls were concrete and lined with boxes. There was nothing else in the room, just like all the others it had been stripped bare. I saw scuff marks and dried blood covering the floor. There was a partial bloody footprint on the floor that walked toward the stairs. I felt a shiver run up my spine as I asked myself the one question I didn't want the answer to. What happened here?

I was starting to feel claustrophobic in the small room until I caught sight of sunlight. There was one window—it was small—but I could climb out of it if I forced myself through. I had a chance to escape, and I wasn't going to let it slip away. I propped boxes in front of the window and lifted myself to the window seal. I tried to push open the small window, but it was no use; I couldn't open the window fully. It got stuck half-way and wouldn't move any further. I would have to be about six years old to fit through that space.

With a heavy sigh, I closed the window and jumped down. I had to have the house put together again before Damien got home, or he'd know I was trying to escape, and I didn't want to know if he would follow through on his threat. My lips twitched slightly at the thought, in a way I wanted him to. Who wouldn't? He had strong features, a handsome face, and a smooth voice that would win over everyone.

He would only have to suggest it, and I would be all over him. Damien was a gentleman, while we were alone, and stunning when I met him. Even now he was mouth-wateringly handsome, but I couldn't let it get to me. I couldn't let him get to me, or this would turn into a plan for isolating us alone for as long as possible. I knew it would be hard because I had growing feelings for him, but I could only hope that it was lust and nothing more.

I heard the sound of gravel crunching under tires and panicked. I quickly ran back upstairs. The wooden stairs creaked loudly under my hasty footsteps. There was a loud slam as he tried to force the door open. I shrank back into the couch with each blow to the door until it slammed forcefully into the wall behind it. Damien's feet stomped around downstairs for a few moments before I heard them travel up toward me. I grabbed a book about a dog off the table in front of me and flipped open to a random page. I read about six lines before Damien ripped the book from my hands and glared down at me.

"What's wrong?"

Damien's answer was slamming a newspaper onto the table next to me. He was shaking with anger. I glanced over to see my face plastered onto the front of the paper.

"It looks like you weren't as unwanted as I thought," Damien growled.

"What do you mean?"

"You're being looked for. Too bad they won't find you soon enough," he said as he stalked off down the stairs again.

"Why is that?"

"Because I won't let them. You're mine," he growled again as he leaned into me. I felt my heart go into overdrive as I fought the urge to latch my fingers in his jet black hair and pull his face down to mine. Luckily, he turned on a heel and stormed off before I could give into my body's temptation.

I picked up the paper to see that I was front news, 'Anna Cowles' daughter kidnapped.' Steve Bennett was listed as a source and then a few rhetorical questions about why Anna Cowles hadn't come out of hiding to locate her daughter. Although, in small print in the lower corner of the page, I could see that my parents had put out a plea to locate me. They may not know that I was kidnapped, but they knew I was missing at least. They would find me, and then I could go home again.

I let out a heavy sigh. Could I get out of this that

easily, or would I end up like the other girls? I wish I had listened to my parents; this is exactly what they had been warning me about.

Chapter 7

"You're mine." The words echoed in my mind every second of the day. From the moment I woke up to the minute I went to sleep. I wish I could have taken them as a threat, other than the words that made my knees weak. I loved the sound of him calling me his. I wanted to hear it all the time and to feel his strong lips on mine.

I sighed to myself knowing that it couldn't happen. I had to get out, but a part of me wanted to be with Damien. He was handsome, funny, seductive, and full of excitement. Too bad I couldn't be with him. He had taken me as a part of Steve's plan to get out of jail; Damien was tainted by Steve.

I just couldn't figure out why he was a part of Steve's plan. What did Damien have to gain? I couldn't see anything, which means I was missing some information. I sighed heavily again as my hand fell on my father's journal. Its leather-bound pages had given me insight to my father's childhood. I finally understood why he lied about his past; he was really lying to himself. It was the only way he could deal with the beatings, the screams of the other girls, and his whole life.

He was kidnapped at the age of ten, but didn't know until Steve let it slip when he brought a little girl home for my mother. He had believed this was just the life he was born in to, but to learn he was taken from his actual family cut him to pieces. He wrote that the only thing that got him through it was my mother. Even though they fought—literally screaming down each other's throats from what he wrote—he said he could only think about the time they kissed. He felt sparks, and he knew he had fallen in love with her. He couldn't understand what was different about her from the other girls. He had been with other girls, one even threw herself at him—needless to say I skipped that part of the journal.

Eventually he understood the only way he could have the love of his life was if they escaped. They had to escape together, along with the new little girl in the family. He didn't mention the girl too much, only said that she was young with blonde hair and wouldn't speak. After that he wrote very minimally; he explained they had a plan of escape and hoped it worked. He wrote he wasn't sure if he would survive the beating Steve was going to give him since Steve had fallen in love with Anna as well. There was just something about her that caused people to fall in love with her; she couldn't help it.

At the end of the entry, he said that would be the last time he would write. The journal had to be hidden, in case Steve found it; he wanted it to be hard to find so he and Anna could be long gone.

"That's so sweet. He was only thinking of mom while he was here," I said silently to myself, as I looked up at the only light upstairs.

My father had accepted his fate of living in his house, but once he knew he had something, or someone, to fight for, he wasn't going to stay. He must have known this whole place from the inside out; too bad he didn't tell me any of that in the book. Maybe then I would have known a way to get out.

He had only made mention of that room I found earlier. He called it a basement, but to me it seemed like more of a cellar. My father said that's where Steve beat him, so the blood wouldn't frighten the new girls Steve brought in. Now I knew what happened in that room, but I still wish I didn't. He did mention it was possible to open the window even wider. He figured out that you could pop the window out of place, but it still wasn't big enough for him. I paused for a moment as I reread that line. You could open the top part of the window by pulling it toward you; it popped out of place.

Without a second thought I grabbed the backpack Damien had given me and stuffed the extra clothes and the journal into it. I quickly ran down the stairs, knowing that Damien was out of the house and I could make as much noise as needed. I skipped stairs two at a time, hope rising in me. I was going to get out. My father had given me the information I needed, and I was going to get out and find a way home. I thought excitedly about seeing my family and friends again after what felt like years. I was finally going to be free again, I thought, as I pried open the door to the basement.

I raced down the stairs to see the only ray of sunshine I had seen since being brought here. I could feel the smile forming on my face as I found the boxes I used last time and positioned them under the window. I opened the lower half of the window by turning the handles. I was immediately hit with a cold breeze from the outside. I shivered at the sudden chill and tried to force the upper part out. It was stuck from the cold and was freezing to the touch.

I finally forced the top part of the window open, and it let in a huge gust of wind that made me shiver. My smile grew larger as I tossed my bag out of the window.

"Why is it so cold?" I asked myself. I removed my hands from the window momentarily and rubbed them together as I continued to crawl out.

"It's cold because it's the middle of November," Damien's dark voice said from behind me.

I froze. I couldn't even turn around to look at him, but I could feel him staring at me. "Is it really?" I asked, as I tried to pull myself fully out of the window but couldn't; my waist was stuck.

"Yes, in fact, I think it's almost Thanksgiving. It's about a week away now," he said, as his footsteps and voice got closer to me.

"So that makes it about two months since I was taken here," I said, as my brain tried to wrap around how I had lost so much time. I didn't think it was more than a week at most. The days were starting to blur together; I wasn't even able to distinguish days from months anymore.

"Roughly. You came with me at the beginning of September, right before starting your senior year of high school," his voice was right behind me now.

"Close the window, Audrey, you'll catch a cold."

"Right." I sighed in defeat as I shut the window. Damien helped me off the boxes and moved away from me, the glare deep set in his eyes.

"Now, explain to me what you were trying to do," he said, as his voice turned dark and threatening.

"Isn't it obvious?" I asked sarcastically. It may not have been my best choice, but it was my defense against whatever Damien had up his sleeve, and I was going to work with what I had.

"It looked like you were trying to escape, but even you have to know that it's stupid."

"I'm not stupid!"

"Then what were you trying to do?" he repeated, as he glared down at me with disdain.

"I was trying to get the air flowing down here. It's stuffy."

"How did you even know about this room?"

"Oh, you didn't? I guess Steve doesn't really like you then." I sneered, as I tried to walk around him to make it back upstairs.

"You're not going anywhere!" he said, grabbing me by the shoulder.

"You can't keep me wherever you want me to be, Damien. I'm not some toy that you can control!"

"You'll do as you're told, Audrey!"

"Oh, because that worked out so well for kids nowadays, right?" I said with a smirk.

"You're just upset you've learned the hard way that your parents were right, and that boyfriend of yours isn't going to magically come and save you," Damien sneered, hitting as low as he could go.

"How dare you bring Mark into this!"

"He doesn't want you. He would be looking for you if he did. You were just some girl to him. He used you as a hook-up and doesn't care that you're gone now! So get over it, because I'm the only one you have left!"

"You're wrong! My parents will come find me!"

"Anna isn't going to come out of hiding. She changed her name and hid to protect herself and her family, including you. If she comes out and tells everyone that she is Anna Cowles, then she'd be swarmed by reporters again and have to suffer the remembrance of what she went through."

"At least she is doing something for her family. What about you? I'm pretty sure you don't have anyone or care about anyone!"

"Shut up, Audrey. You don't know what you're talking about!" he screamed. I clearly hit a chord with him.

"You only have Steve, is that it? Is that why you work with him? You're related somehow!"

"I'm not related to that monster!"

"Judging from your reaction, you are. You're embarrassed, and now what? You're trying to help him get out of jail? What is he to you? A brother? An uncle?" I prodded as I watched the anger in Damien's eyes increase with each word I spoke.

I instantly regretted it as Damien grabbed me by the shoulders and shoved me against the wall. It forced me to look at him and took away whatever power I thought I had.

"I'm not related to that man. I don't know him, I am not his family, and I am not helping him because I want to! I only have a sister, no parents left, no extended family, and as much as I hate hurting girls, if you continue to talk about this, I will slam your head against the wall. You have no idea what you're talking about; you're jumping to the wrong conclusions. Now get out of my sight before I do something I'll regret," he said, pushing me from the wall and behind him.

"Damien...I'm..."

"Get out of my sight, Audrey! I don't want to see you again! Get out of here! Go to your room!" he roared, sending me up the stairs in terror. I had clearly hit a button that I didn't want to hit again.

Chapter 8

I could feel Damien's stare burning a hole into my back. He has been standing at the entranceway to the common room while I was reading a book titled, *A Dog's life: The Autobiography of a Stray*. When I first picked it up from the table after Damien's first day out of the house, it had layers of dust that made me disgusted to have to hold it, but for some reason I felt a connection to the book.

"You'll have to get used to being here, Audrey," Damien's husky voice growled. I tightened my thighs to control the desires that his voice sent through my system before I responded. We had been fighting for what felt like weeks, but without the natural sunlight and clocks, I didn't know how much time had actually passed. I had spent a whole day in my room just to be away from him; I was transfixed by those photos on the wall. Each of those girls was trapped here, including my mother and my father, and now I was here. I could only hope this wouldn't become a family legacy. That is if I ever got out of here to have children.

"I won't be here long. You saw the paper; people

know I'm gone," I said with a smirk on my lips, knowing that I was pushing Damien's buttons.

"That's what you think."

"Damien, can you seriously think they won't check here if they think Steve has a copycat? This will probably be the first place they look."

"I know," he said nonchalantly, but I could hear the smile in his words.

"Then why aren't you worried? You'll be arrested for kidnapping."

"You came with me willingly because you were hoping to have sex again, Audrey. Is that a lie?" he asked, as he took a few steps toward me. I could feel my chest tightening with anticipation; I bit my lip to stop the urge to reach out and touch him.

"I came with you because I didn't want to go back to my parents," I said strongly, as he stopped behind the couch.

"Then why didn't you run off to that boyfriend of yours?" Damien whispered in my ear, sending shivers up my spine.

"Because we can't legally be dating, remember?" I forced myself to face him to show my lack of emotion. His dark eyes bore into mine as he tried to find something hidden in my gaze.

"I think it's because you liked me better."

"Your ego is huge. For all you know we could have been fighting."

"Fighting after having sex with him at a party, and getting caught by Officer Sparks?" he suggested with such accuracy that I spun in the seat to face him.

It was a big mistake. His face was mere inches

away from mine, so close that the slightest motion forward would send us into a kiss. I bit my lip to prevent those thoughts from taking over. I was starting to have strong feelings for Damien, and if they got too strong, I would never leave him.

"How did you know about that?"

"It's amazing the things you tell me when you're drunk, sweetheart," he said, tucking a strand of my hair behind my ear. I felt my breath catch in my throat and force swallowed it to hide the urge to kiss him as hard as I could with everything in me.

"I'll be sure not to do it again," I sneered, as I plopped back down onto the sofa and opened my book again.

"Good, because when we make love, I want you to be completely sober," he said as he walked away laughing.

"It won't happen!" I called, as his footsteps retreated down the stairs. "It won't," I restated to reassure myself. I couldn't let it happen, but it didn't mean I didn't want it to happen. Every time he spoke to me or looked into my eyes, I had the overwhelming urge to kiss him.

He was right; I did want him. I had come willingly, but I was being forced to stay. How had my mom made it through this? Of course, I didn't have to deal with any of the abuse she had, or at least what I knew of the case, but those could just be horror stories told by the news. My parents never discussed it, as if they had never been a part of Steve Bennett's life. They ignored it so that they could live normal lives afterward. They moved and changed my mom's name so that they could be safe, and so I could be safe. I sighed heavily as I thought about how rude I had been to my parents when I found out.

I called them liars, but worst of all I said I hated them, and I never wanted to see them again. All that was because of anger, from the lies, the laws, and the arrests, but now I wanted nothing more than to be back at home. I had even been mean to James, and he was only doing his job. He took care of me like his own daughter. It hurt just as much to see me act out as it did for them. James had known my parents since they got married, and must have moved with them to Wilmington in order to know them that long.

It suddenly made sense. They were so close, even though they never recalled how they met or previous times together. They were brought together by this event—but how? What would have brought them together? There was no way Steve would have taken a police officer, much less a chief of police. James did have a daughter, now that I thought about it, Jessi Sparks. She's my godmother and went to college at Appalachian State, about four hours away from Wilmington, and then to another college so she could work for the FBI after she graduated. Jessi was even more closed off about her childhood than my parents were.

My parents would talk about it, of course there were obvious gaps and lies to make up for the time spent in the house, but they would tell me stories about their childhood. My father eventually just stopped answering and let my questions fall to deaf ears, but Jessi never tried to come up with a lie. It was almost like she couldn't lie, so she never responded. She laughed whenever I asked her about her childhood and then changed the topic.

Does that mean Jessi was here too, or was it all a coincidence? James and Jessi could have met my parents before they were kidnapped, or after they were recovered. My parents would have had to stay in Virginia in order to testify in Steve's case. They could have met James and Jessi after the case, too. It was just a coincidence, I said to myself, as I turned the page and had a piece of paper fall into my lap. It was worn by time and from being stuffed between the pages. I glanced behind me to make sure Damien had really left, and hadn't been standing there watching me as he often did, before I opened it.

In case you come back here Anna and I'm gone, I hope he didn't catch you first off, but I also want to tell you that I love you. I am going to meet you and Jessi in Charleston as soon as I can, but I know this beating is going to hurt the worst of any before. So don't expect me for a while, and in case he caught you, just know I love you and I will find Jessi. I'm sorry, I will try to send help, but you know how cops are... Good-bye Anna.

"Well, there goes the coincidence theory," I sighed, as footsteps started pounding on the stairs behind me.

I quickly stuffed the note back into the book and shut it tight as Damien came upstairs. His chest was heaving, and his eyes were filled with worry that sent fear through my body. I wasn't supposed to feel anything for him, but his worry gave me heartache. Crap, what was I doing to myself? I was falling in love with him.

"We have to get out of here!" he said, going into my room and starting to rummage through the clothes he had given me.

"What's going on?" I asked as I walked over to him. He was busy throwing the clothes he had gotten me into a bag.

"They came sooner than I thought. I thought for sure I had another week, but it turns out I don't. We have to leave, Audrey."

"People are coming to get me?"

"Yes, but I'm not letting them take you. I can't, otherwise..." Damien let the sentence fall as he continued to slam things into the bag.

"Otherwise what?"

"Nothing! Just help me pack!"

"No, I won't help! They're coming to get me, Damien. Why would I help you?"

"Because your life depends on it like mine does," he said with a shaky voice.

"What?" I asked curiously, I couldn't have heard him correctly. How did my life depend on it?

"Never mind, Audrey! Just get out of here, I'll come get you when I'm done packing—we have to leave," Damien yelled in a panic. Now I understood my dad's comment about my mother and him screaming down each other's throats in this house. It was bound to happen, they couldn't get their feelings straight, and it came back at them as anger. "Just go, Audrey, please. I'll come get you," he said, as he continued to pack things tightly into a bag.

I just nodded and made my way into the other rooms. I accepted that I was going to be moved; it would be easier for me to escape when we were moving and he was distracted. I just had to time it right, and I'd be back home in no time. I just had to wait, but why was Damien in such a sudden rush to leave? What did he really have to lose?

He wasn't going to tell me anytime soon, I could tell. Maybe I could get that out of him too, if I played my cards right. I felt a mischievous smile curl my lips; I was going to escape, one way or another.

Chapter 9

I had never been in the other rooms before, and if I hadn't known better I would have guessed no one had ever been in them either. I stepped into one room and the bed was made, as if it had never been slept in. The walls were bare, and the only furniture was a desk and a bookshelf. The desk was completely bare. There was nothing on it or in it except a slip of paper with the drawing of a black dog. At least I think it was a dog; it had a circle for a head, long floppy ears and a stick body.

"This was your father's room," Damien said from behind me.

"Well, I guess my father isn't much of an artist," I stated, as I started to look through the bookshelf.

There were books stuffed into every possible spot that my dad could have found. The books seemed to progress as he aged, but suddenly stopped in his early teens. There was nothing past that to challenge him in reading; something caused him to not get any more books, and he was forced to stop.

"Now I know why he always forced me to read.

He couldn't, so he made sure that I could."

"Sounds like a good guy. Now, let's go," Damien growled as he came into the room.

"I just started looking."

"Correction, you just started learning about your parents for the first time, and now you actually care about them because you realize your life isn't so bad. Now get up, we have to go!" he said, pulling me up off the ground and from the bedroom.

"What's gotten into you?" I questioned, as Damien pulled me down the stairs and toward the front door.

"Stay," he ordered, as he dropped a bag by my feet and stormed off. He stalked toward a hidden door on the other side of the stairs. I could hear him rummaging around in the room, knocking stuff over, and crashing them to the ground.

My feet carried me to the noise before my mind could process what I was doing. Each time I tried to look while Damien was out, the door was locked and wouldn't open no matter how much I tried to force it. I felt as if it was supposed to keep me out, as well as keep whoever was inside trapped. I stepped inside to see the room at its fullest. There was a king size bed with white sheets and a rose petal heart in the center of the bed. A sheer white canopy cascaded over the bed and provided minimal light with the string lights that were wrapped around the bedposts. The rest of the rose petals were scattered over the room and accompanied by more candles that were meant to set the scene for a romantic night.

"What are you doing in here?" Damien yelled

once he turned to see me standing in the doorway.

"I was just..."

"I told you to stay put, Audrey, it's for your own good!" Damien cried out, as he tried to push me out of the room.

"You're keeping me locked up. That's not for my own good, Damien!" I said, side-stepping him and walking him into the room.

"Audrey, stop!" Damien shouted, as I felt cool metal clamp onto my ankle, holding me in that spot.

"What is this?" I cried, as I unsuccessfully attempted to remove my foot from the trap.

"I tried telling you. There are some places he warned me not to go to in the house, and in some towns. He booby-trapped them in case I didn't listen. He's hiding his secrets as well as he can. Even the police couldn't get past them while searching the house."

"What's the point?" I asked, just as a loud crackling reached my ears. I turned to see a small fire brewing in the corner of the room.

"We have to get out of here. His plan was never to let you live. He only wants Anna," Damien explained, as he smoothly released the trap and led me out of the room.

"What are you talking about?" An explosion of fire covered up my cry as Damien's hand clasped onto mine.

"There's no time to explain! Just come with me!" he ordered, as he pulled me from the room. He picked up the bag and tried to force open the door, but couldn't open it. The door opened slightly, but slammed shut again. We weren't able to get out, and the fire was rapidly expanding from behind us.

"Damien, hurry up!"

"I'm trying!" he grunted as he tried to force the door open. "It's stuck!"

Behind us the fire hit another accelerant and exploded loudly. The force shook the floor and caused the ceiling above us to rip apart. Wood splinters and drywall showered us as smoke filled the air.

"Cover your mouth, Audrey! Don't breathe the smoke in!" Damien warned, as he continued to try to pry the door open.

There was a continuous pulling at the door as the fire continued to spread. When Damien finally forced the door open and shoved me outside. I tripped down the stairs and landed face first in the dirt. My head was spinning as heat started to scorch my back, but I didn't want to move.

"Audrey, you're on fire. Roll over!" Damien said as he rolled me over as roughly as he could.

I rolled a few feet and scraped my face and hands from the gravel. I came to a stop on my stomach and then felt something hitting my back lightly. I glanced up to see Damien hitting me with his shirt, so that the flames would die, but my gaze fell on the tightening of his muscles with each swing of his shirt. The way his arms flexed as he drew them back to let the shirt hit the flames. I couldn't stop watching his abs tighten as he brought the shirt down. Every movement was elegant and mouthwatering.

"Stop!" I said loudly, mostly to make myself stop thinking about Damien like that. I had to stay focused, play my cards right, and escape. I needed to stay focused; my life depended on it. "I'm fine."

Damien's face went from worried to angry in a flash, making a stop at shocked along the way as he forced me off the ground. He roughly took my arm so that he could walk me to the car.

"What are you doing, Damien? Take me home now!" I ordered.

"I just saved your life, twice! You don't get it, Audrey. Life here is better than it was back home!"

"How so? I could be having sex with Mark right now," I stated, annoying him even more as he shoved me in the car.

"You really think that boy is looking for you?"

"My parents are. So he would be, too."

"You're ignorant." Damien scalded as he slammed the door, closing off conversation for now as he packed the car for departure.

I watched as the house, slowly at first then more rapidly, came ablaze. The glass of the windows shattered; the wood of the house caught flame quickly and slowly turned black. The wood was accelerating it somehow; probably another one of Steve's booby-traps. Were we supposed to make it out alive? Damien and I could have been killed. Was that all a part of Steve's plan? Damien slid into the car without a word and turned it on. He didn't even look at me, just silently started the long drive toward the road.

"What's going on?" I asked curiously. The sudden change in demeanor had been enough to make me cooperate, but the house being set on fire was something I didn't expect.

"Your mother surprised him. He didn't think that she would come out of hiding to find you, but he was hoping," he said as he switched on the radio, and the reporter told the world that there was shocking news.

"*The* Anna Cowles comes out of hiding to save her daughter, and Steve Bennett claims that he knows who did it and where to find them."

My neck cracked, searing me with pain as my hand went to the burning area, as I looked at Damien. His hands holding onto the steering wheel with such force I could see the white of his knuckles. He looked as if he didn't know what to do. His eyes were darting frantically from left to right as he tried to decide where to go. He turned right and took off like a shot out of a gun without a second thought. I knew nothing about where we were going or what was planned. According to the reports and stories I heard as a child, and the ones I read from Garrett's journal, Steve never took the girls out of the house.

That's when I realized I wasn't a part of the kidnapping of Anna Cowles. I was in for something much worse.

Chapter 10

Damien drove for hours, with no direction in mind, but he was clearly avoiding towns. The house had exploded in a loud pop when we pulled out of the driveway; I could only imagine how much attention it was getting. I had fallen asleep on the car ride to the house, but now I had to pay attention to where we were going. If I was going to escape, I had to know the area as best as I could. But this was nothing like South Carolina, and the temperature was drastically different.

"Here, I got you a jacket while I was out the other day," Damien said, for the first time breaking the silence between us.

He searched with one hand in the back of the car and pulled out a black winter coat. Without a glance in my direction he placed it in my lap and continued to drive. I stared at him for a few moments before I put on the coat and continued to shiver in silence as trees whizzed by and the sky started to darken. I continually glanced toward Damien as he drove. I couldn't understand how he seemed so calm after what just happened. The house was on fire, burning rapidly, and he just acted as if it didn't happen. What did he mean that Steve didn't plan to keep me alive? I had a strong feeling that Damien wasn't supposed to get me out of there, but the door was stuck, so was he supposed to die too? He did save my life—not that he'd hear me admit that—and I was thankful he did. Now if I could go back home and forget about this.

"Anna Cowles is speaking out against having a stay of execution in Steve Bennett's case, even though her own daughter was taken by a kidnapper and he claims to know who it is," a reporter stated over the airwaves.

"I sure wouldn't be able to do that, Chet," another reporter said. "I'd do anything to get my kid back home."

"Even let a mass kidnapper and murderer out of jail for a few days?"

"If that's what it took. Guards would surround him while he was out, I don't see the risk that Anna is talking about. He wouldn't be able to escape, so what's the problem?"

"He did kill six or so cops when being brought into custody when he was finally captured. Anna was there, and is trying to make sure he doesn't have the chance again."

"I still would let him out to help–" Damien shut off the radio with a look of disgust on his face. I could hear the sigh of frustration escape his lips.

"You should just take me home, Damien. They won't know it was you, no one will believe Steve, and you'll be off the hook."

"Someone clearly believed Steve, otherwise they

wouldn't be putting out the story."

"So he's just going to accuse a random person?" I retorted a little more rudely than I had meant for it to come out.

"You don't know the whole story, so just shut up," Damien stated in a growl. There was something he wasn't telling me, actually it was probably a lot that he wasn't telling me. I didn't understand how it all connected to Steve, my family, or myself. It didn't make any sense that this man was helping a man he didn't seem to like, or maybe he did and hid it. Damien seemed to be neutral, but there were times when I thought that he actually hated Steve. So the question really became, why was he helping Steve? There had to be some reason for this man helping a psychopath. How had Steve gotten Damien to go along with it?

"Then tell me the whole story."

"You don't need to know."

"You have me trapped in a car, going who knows where, I think it's my business."

"Well, you're wrong. You've already been missing about two months, I knew I'd have to move you, but I wasn't planning on it so soon. I have a few places we are going to stop, and then finally make it to where we're supposed to be."

"Where are we going?" I asked, for the moment dropping the topic of taking me home. I was growing frustrated with the same debate that we had been having for the last two months. I hadn't even realized so much time had gone by.

"You don't need to know."

"Then tell me what I need to know or can know,"

I spat, annoyed that I knew nothing, but Damien knew everything.

"You only need to know that you and I will be together forever," he said with a seductive smile. "It will be of your own freewill, too."

"In your dreams," I scoffed, as I whipped my head around to look out the window at the unfamiliar landscape.

"Come on, Audrey. You can't tell me that you didn't find me attractive when I picked you up from that bar."

"I didn't find you attractive," I stated with an even voice, impressing myself with how easy it was to lie. "Especially after you kidnapped me."

"You came willingly," Damien said, as I instigated the debate that would carry on until this was over, and possibly after I got home if word got around that I went willingly with him from the bar.

"You're holding me against my will."

"Do you even know the meaning of kidnap?" Damien asked with a smirk on his face that told me my logic wasn't as accurate as I hoped it to be.

"I know that it's to be held against my will, as I am."

"Well you're partially right at least, but in a few weeks you'll warm up to the idea of being with me."

"You mean Stockholm Syndrome? That sounds like a completely free choice," I asked with sarcastic humor in my tone.

Damien said nothing; he just turned to glare at me. I could see the frustration in his eyes, along with an emotion he was trying to hide. The frustration was clear, but clouded by worry and fear. The fear worried me; I thought this was all part of the plan, but clearly that wasn't the case. Damien hadn't expected the fire; he had rushed to get us out of the house and save me. Steve didn't plan for that—I wasn't who he wanted.

Damien looked away from me and back toward our lonely stretch of road. There was nothing around us except for trees. There were no signs to tell me what we were near, or street signs, unless you lived in the area you wouldn't know where you were and wouldn't know which way to go.

All I wanted was to find a way home—somehow, and then beg my parents for forgiveness. I shouldn't have said I hated them; it may be the last thing they ever hear me say.

Chapter 11

"I can't wait any longer, Audrey," a dark voice said filling my ears. I glanced up to see Steve Bennett standing above me as he looked at me with lust in his eyes.

"Please, don't!" I cried out as he played with the waistband of my shorts.

"Now I can get these things off, finally," he said with a sigh, as he popped the button of my shorts.

"Please don't do this!" I screamed.

"Shut up!" he ordered. The sound of ripping cotton met my ears. My shirt split in pieces, turned to tatters in a matter of seconds, and thrown aside like garbage.

I heard him moan, "Ready, Audrey?"

"Please stop!" I screamed as pain shot through my body.

I shot up and banged my head against the roof of the car Damien had me cramped into. My hands crashed to my head as I winced in pain. A low hiss escaped through my teeth, and again when the seatbelt pulled me backward into my seat. I glanced over to see Damien with a worried look on his face, more like horrified. I could smell burnt rubber and could see the smoke coming from around us. It must have been a rough stop.

"What's wrong?" Damien asked, his face stuck in the same contorted position of fear. He didn't take his eyes off me as I glanced around the car to make sure I was safe. I was still buckled in, with Damien driving, and luckily no Steve anywhere in sight. I put my hand to my chest as I tried to slow the rapid heartbeat, but it was no use, the dream had caused more than just fear. It reminded me what I was running from.

"Sorry, I had a bad dream," I said, glancing at the tamper-proof door lock to see if I could escape just as the car started.

"What was it about?" Damien asked picking up the conversation as he continued down the road. I guess he had been driving in silence for so long, that he was looking for something to talk about.

"Steve Bennett," I answered curtly, not wishing to explain that I had seen him. I knew the case as well as anyone; I just never dreamed about it. It felt so real, and that was terrifying to think about.

"What about him?"

"I don't know really," I said with a long drawn out sigh. "It was really unclear, I felt as if I was my mom. I could see the attack from her point of view, and it was awful."

"What do you mean?"

"Why do you care?" I sneered at his sudden interest in me. He had been ignoring me lately; his moods would change faster than the weather in a mountain town. He never wanted to talk to me, why should that change?

"Like I have anything else to do right now," he growled as he glared at me, taking his eyes off the road. I suddenly felt uncomfortable having him watch me, it only reminded me of Steve's gaze during the dream.

"If you want something to do, you could look at the road, or pull over."

"Fine, I'm looking at the road now," he said maneuvering so that he could look at the road, and me at the same time. It looked more as if he was about to fall out of the car if he wasn't careful, and it didn't make me feel any better.

"Fine, it was about Steve Bennett. It was as if I was living through an experience that my mom had, but like I was living through it. It's so hard to explain."

"You were living an experience because you compare me to Steve Bennett. Don't worry, I don't plan on hurting you," Damien said, placing his hand on my leg and patting me lightly.

"I think you already have," I scoffed, shoving his hand off of me and moving as far away as I could from him in the tight space.

"You'll grow to love me. It won't be hard since you already find me attractive," he said in a tone that sent me into an angry frenzy.

"I don't know what gave you that idea, but—"

"You struggle to control yourself around me, when I get close to you it's hard to focus, but you try to look away from me. You stare at me, watch me, and I know what you're thinking when you do. It's all in your eyes, your breathing gives it away too. Especially when I'm so close to you that you can't control how you react.

"So? That doesn't mean anything!" I shrieked in annoyance as Damien stopped the car again.

"I know that you get tempted when I'm close to you like when I leaned close you on the couch. I could see it in your eyes that you wanted to kiss me, but you were too proud and had to look away when you knew I was winning," he said with a smile as his hand moved up my thigh slightly, making my body tingle with anticipation.

I felt my breath catch as his hand slowly moved up my thigh. I could feel my lip starting to hurt under the bite of my teeth. My back was starting to arch in hope for another night with Damien. Even though I disliked him for taking me from home to help Steve, I couldn't ignore the effect he had on me. He was attractive, and I had growing feelings toward him. He leaned closer, his lips only inches from mine. I leaned forward, but before I could kiss him he pulled away.

"I could say I told you, but I think you found out for yourself," Damien said pulling his hand away and leaving my body crying out for more.

I really needed to escape, because if I didn't I would let myself give in to him and never leave. I would get to have amazing experiences with him; I would almost trade my freedom for that. Almost, but I couldn't do that if Steve was going to be let loose again. I couldn't give in to temptation, until I knew Steve would be dead. I just had to remember if Steve got out, we would all be in danger.

"Well, you're wrong. Now stop touching me," I

ordered, pushing him away from me.

"Why do you have a problem with me touching you? I think you rather enjoy it from the reaction you just gave," Damien stated with a chuckle as he leaned back against the door. There was a subtle click of the door lock disengaging. Damien didn't hear it or ignored it, until I pushed open my door and took off running.

I heard him yell as I raced to the trees. I didn't turn back, I had to take my chance, and with any luck I was as tough as my mom, and would make it back to them to tell them how sorry I was.

Chapter 12

I skirted through the trees before Damien got out of the car. There was no clear path anywhere so I cut through the brush. The forest was thick with foliage and brush; it was almost too difficult to walk through. I had to get away from him, then I could focus on finding a way home. Damien's voice followed after me, he sounded amused as he looked for me. What's so amusing about me getting away from him? Didn't he need me for his plans?

I raced past trees and fallen logs that looked like an animal had raked its claws along it. I stopped for a few seconds to catch my breath and listened to see if Damien was close to me. There was no sound for a while; it was eerily silent. It was the silence that brought shivers to my spine. With silence came unknown; I had no idea where Damien was or if he was still following me. The silence could mean that he stopped following me. I could have lost him, or he gave up, but I had a feeling that he wasn't the kind of person to give up. He would chase me until he was sure I was either dead or he had me again.

"There you are, Audrey," Damien said, as he

slapped his hands on my shoulders to hold me into place.

"Yep, here I am," I said with a nervous tone. How had I not heard him coming? How had he managed to sneak up on me?

"You shouldn't have run away, you don't know the woods well enough to escape."

"I don't need to escape. I just need to get away from you," I said smartly, as I tried to move away from him again.

"I think you've already learned that running from me doesn't do you any good, Audrey. So please, for both our sakes stop trying to run away," Damien said with a frustrated tone.

"It's worth a shot, right?" I said with a smirk forming on my lips.

"If you say so, sweetheart," Damien said with a smile on his lips. It was almost as if he found it cute to call me that, but I think he just found it funny to push my buttons.

"Don't call me that."

"If I stop calling you that will you stop running?" Damien asked in a suddenly annoyed tone.

"Yes, if you stop calling me sweetheart I'll stop running," I lied smoothly. I needed to get him focused on something else or at least in a better position so I could try to escape again. He looked skeptical, but he wasn't in the mood for an argument because he quickly moved on.

"I'm glad you've gotten it out of your system. Let's go," Damien said, sticking his hand out for me to take.

"Sorry, I have other plans," I said, as I took his hand and lifted my knee into his groin.

Damien automatically fell to the ground in agonizing pain. I took off running once my knee met its mark. I kept running until I was sure Damien was a safe distance from me, when I couldn't hear his groans. I slouched to the ground beside a large tree, my chest was threatening to crush my heart. I was heaving, hard short breaths due to the cold temperatures. I suddenly wished that I had run in high school instead of joining the swim team. Being able to swim long distances wasn't going to do much for me here, but being able to run fast and far would have helped.

As I continued to walk, I could feel the brush digging into my legs, but I had to be quiet to hope that I would remain hidden. My foot snagged on a raised root, and I tripped into the dirt. That's when I heard laughter, maniacal and crazed, coming from behind me.

"Who's there?" I asked worriedly.

When no one answered, I decided it was time to keep going. I didn't know who else would be out here except Damien, and I hoped he was the only other person out here. I ran through branches, twigs, thorns, leaves, and continually tripped over ingrown roots and rocks. The sun had almost completely vanished in the darkening twilight, giving off an orange glow around the trees and through the branches. This would be the last visible light of the day; I would be sent into darkness. I glanced around the area to see if there was any cover I could use to sleep for the night.

There were a few branches laying askew on the ground, crafting habitats for the animals. There were dead branches and tall bushes littering the ground, making it difficult to walk through the brush. I could hear animal claws scratching into the earth around me as they seemed to get closer and closer. There was a growl, here and there, while pairs of yellow eyes watched every one of my movements.

"I'm going to be fine here," I said to reassure myself, as I found a small opening under a tree.

I reluctantly crawled into the small opening and curled up. I could hear the nocturnal animals begin to stir while the others went to sleep. The claws were raking into the sides of the trees and in the soil around me. For a while I thought I heard footsteps and a few times they got really close to me. I watched carefully as I fell into an uneasy sleep.

When I woke up, the sun was almost in the middle of the sky. It made me wonder if Damien was already out looking for me or if he had given up the search. I could only hope for the latter so I could escape and be free of him as I crawled out of my hole. My scream pierced the cool November day when a hand grabbed my shoulder. There was something different about this, it was rougher and angrier; it wasn't Damien.

"It's funny really, you look so much like your mother. You even took almost the same route your mother did when she tried to leave me," a dark heavy voice said from behind me. I was frozen with fear, I couldn't move—I couldn't think. "You will turn to look at me when I talk to you," the voice said, as he shoved me to the ground for not obeying.

As he stood over me I saw the person of my nightmares. He was what I grew to fear, and what I should have run from, but I was frozen where I fell. I felt my breath quiver as I tried to process who I was seeing, I was looking into the green eyes of Steve Bennett. Suddenly, being trapped with Damien and fighting the urge to kiss him wasn't so bad.

"Steve Bennett, they let you out of jail?"

"Of course, who wouldn't want to find you? They want to make sure they caught the right man, and they have to make an example out of my copycat so that more won't step forward. I was shocked when they let me come with them, but I need your mother, not you. The only way for that to happen is to take you with me."

He reached out for me and I screamed until the lining of my throat tore. I scrambled to get my footing, but before I could run off, he grabbed me roughly and pulled me toward him. His hands latched onto me, and I knew I wasn't going to be able to escape as easily as I had done with Damien.

My life was officially over.

Chapter 13

I swallowed my fear as I tried to process what to do next. Steve Bennett was the most feared criminal of the last century, and I knew the things he would do to me. Even if Steve hadn't admitted to the rape and kidnapping on national television, my father's journal had told me all about his actions, and that meant I had to escape if I wanted a chance to get home unharmed.

"Come, Anna."

"I'm not Anna! Why do you keep calling me that?" I cried as he roughly pushed me forward.

"You look so much like your mother. So much alike in fact, that if I can't have her, I'll think of keeping you. What do you have to say to that?" he said, as his hands started to travel my body. Shivers traveled up my spine, and not the ones that Damien gave me, these were fear driven.

"I'd rather not!" I cried, as I pulled out of his hold and ran as fast as I could.

I could hear Steve's maniacal laughter as I raced away. The thorns and branches were cutting deeply into my legs and stomach as I sped through the trees. I hopped over fallen trees, trying to escape, but the whole time I could hear Steve talking to me. He was always just a few steps behind me.

"Audrey, if it hurts your feelings so much, I will call you by your name instead of your mother's." He was following me no matter where I went, and I knew he would never stop. He was obsessed, and that would mean I would have to keep running.

I hid behind a tree as Steve got closer to me. I listened to his footsteps as they traced around me. He was beating around the bush, literally. His voice continued to drift over me. He was close by, and I realized that I wasn't in the best hiding spot now. He would find me; he always found his target.

"Your mother and I had a wonderful time together. At that time I didn't need an apprentice to bring me girls, but I wasn't even planning on having you come to meet me. Why are you here?" Steve pondered as he passed by my hiding spot.

I shoved my hands into my pockets as I breathed a sigh of relief. My hand jammed into a crumpled piece of paper, which unfolded to reveal a map. The map showed towns—Charleston, Harrisonburg, and a few others that were small in comparison, with circles around their names. There was a large red star and a note above it that said 'here's where you'll get out' in messy handwriting. Was this Damien's handwriting? Had he meant for me to escape? I glanced at the map and tried to match it to the landscape around me, but I needed a road to figure out just were I was.

I started running back toward the road that I had escaped from Damien on, but the second I left my hiding spot Steve grabbed hold of me. He took the map from my hands and forced me to turn around to look into the dark green eyes that caused my fear to spike.

"How did you get a map?" Steve asked. I froze momentarily before kneeing him as I had done to Damien and speeding off again. Once I hit the road, I was able to look at the map. Charleston was the closest to me, and then it was off to Harrisonburg to head south for home. There was a low chuckle behind me, I knew that meant Steve was coming. I had to take off again. I turned on my heels, and raced through the trees until I was stopped once again by Steve Bennett. How was he always able to find me?

"You're following the same paths as the other girls and don't even know it," he said with a smirk.

"Then I guess I'm going to have to think of another way to get back home," I said smartly.

"You could, but I can't let you go because I need you to get your mother back. My bastard of a son took her from me and now I will take her back. You for her, fair trade in that case," Steve said with a knowing smile.

"What do you want from my mom?"

"I want my wife back, but it looks as if my apprentice is trying to prevent it. I was afraid this would happen."

"Afraid what would happen?" I asked, trying to buy time so I could escape.

"That he would fall for you. Your mother had the same trait, and I regret falling into that trap. Now it seems that Damien has made the same mistake. It's a pity. I had to blackmail him into this, and he still failed. At least, he did give me a pretty new girl," Steve said, as he reached out and touched my face.

I cringed at his touch, obviously hurting his feelings. His hand swung back and landed on my cheek with a loud smack. I let out a yelp of pain at the force of the hit. I stumbled, and then ran out of Steve's reach. I ran through the thickest part of the forest, it got so dense at one point I tripped on a tree root, or what I thought was a tree root. My face smacked against the dirt and I looked up to see Damien kneeling in front of me. His index finger was up against his lips as he tried to tell me to keep silent.

"Keep quiet. I'm going to get you out of here."

"Why?"

"I said keep quiet," Damien said, slapping his hand over my mouth as Steve walked past us.

We waited for what felt like hours before Damien lifted me off the ground and pulled me out of the woods. He dragged me through the over growth, the dead plants tangled around my feet and tripped me onto the cold hard ground.

"That was smooth," Damien whispered with a sarcastic tone as I tripped for the fourth time since he found me.

"Shut up," I whispered back.

"Don't be rude. I am saving your life for the third time."

"Why did you save her life so many times, Damien? She was supposed to die in that house. It was planned so that she could never be found," Steve said from behind us, making my skin crawl.

84

"I wasn't going to let you kill this girl just to get your way Bennett. It's not worth killing innocent people," Damien said forcefully as he pulled me behind his back for protection.

"I think it's because you fell in love with her. How else would she get a map? How else would she escape my old house? I set it to blow after you left, and she went wandering in the house. That means that you got her out, and that you've been taking care of her. It's a pity, without her gone, or Anna with me, you'll never get the information you wanted," Steve said with a grimace on his face.

"I'll find out one way or another, even if I have to keep searching on my own. I didn't agree to harm or kill her," Damien said forcefully.

"You agreed to do whatever I asked, so you could find out about your sister," Steve growled. "I guess your sister's fate will never be known."

"Your sister?" I asked from behind Damien. "He knows your sister?"

"Oh, you didn't tell the love of your life about why you kidnapped her?" Steve asked. "Maybe because you had already given up on finding your sister, you love Audrey, and couldn't tell her the truth because it would guilt her into staying with you. Well, now you don't have a choice. I'll be taking Audrey and trading her for her mother. You're done here," Steve stated, as he leaned down and grabbed me roughly by the shoulder.

"Let me go!" I screamed in terror.

"You can't have her!" Damien yelled, as he grabbed me by the waist and pulled me out of Steve's hold. Damien quickly threw me over his shoulder and carried me out of the thick forest foliage. I could hear yelling and screaming as Damien sprinted out of the forest with me over his shoulder.

"Damien! Put me down!"

"I will when we get out of these woods. I can't let him take you!" Damien answered, his voice laced with fear and worry.

"But we are out of the woods!" I said as I watched the dirt turn to pavement.

"Right, sorry. Get in the car, we have to get out here. Don't say another word until we are gone. I don't know how he keeps finding you, but let's stay quiet," Damien said, pushing me into the car and he slid in, instantly starting the car.

We sped off quickly, the tires squealed, probably making tire marks on the road, and Steve's laughter echoed in my ears. Damien drove as if there was a cop car chasing after us. My father's journal had said not to trust cops; they were in on it with Steve. It made me wonder if Damien knew that. Just when I was about to ask, we turned a sharp corner to see Steve standing on the other side of the road, just waiting. My questions would have to wait, for now we needed to escape Steve. We were trapped in a dangerous chase with Steve Bennett, while I was working with the guy that I had feelings for, but who had been working with Steve Bennett.

Something is seriously wrong with me.

Chapter 14

Damien pulled onto a dirt road and swept a cloud of dust over the car. The road was bumpy. I hit my head on the roof of the car, was slammed into the door, and the seatbelt was tight around my body. Damien finally came to stop, and I flung myself out of the car to be on solid ground.

"Thank God, land!" I said, as I raised my hands up to the sky and then fell to the dirt.

"Please, don't be a drama queen, Audrey," Damien said rolling his eyes as he walked by.

"You drive like a maniac!"

"Just get up and shut up about my driving. I got you away from Steve, you should be thankful. That's the third time I've saved your life," Damien said, lifting me off the ground and turning me toward a one-story farmhouse.

"We could have died!"

"Either way we could have died, Audrey. Just get inside before someone hears you and calls the cops," Damien said, opening the screen door and unlocking the wooden door behind it.

"Where are we anyway?" I asked, following him

into the house.

"We are at the house I planned to be at before you got out of the car," Damien said, slamming the door shut.

"You mean before you let me go, right?" I asked as Damien tried to walk further into the house. He stopped suddenly and turned to face me with a confused expression on his face.

"I didn't let you go. You ran off."

"You unlocked the car. You gave me a map to escape with. You gave me a coat for the cold weather, and you gave up chasing me rather quickly," I asserted as I stepped closer to Damien.

He stood his ground and didn't answer right away. In fact, he turned around again and continued to walk through the house without saying a word. I followed him and waited for him to answer, but he didn't. I had to push the topic if I was going to get any answers out of him.

"You let me escape on purpose, why?"

"I didn't let you escape. You just did and you eluded me long enough so that I didn't want to be in the woods at night."

"You gave me a map."

"I had the map and must have left it in the coat," Damien said, pushing aside all my statements.

I had connected the dots, it took about two months, but everything was starting to make sense. Damien didn't seem like a criminal, and that's because he wasn't. He was helping Steve Bennett, but he was doing it for a reason. Damien was looking for his sister, who Steve must have taken. What I couldn't figure out was why Damien needed to help Steve to find where his sister was. All the bodies had been discovered, unless there were more than thirteen girls. Thirteen bodies had been discovered, but only twelve bodies had been found. All the bodies had technically been dug up, but one was only an arm—no body. Since the arm was decayed, they assumed animals or something had taken the body. There was still one girl unaccounted for, and that's who Damien was looking for—his sister.

In order to find his sister he needed Steve. He must have gone to visit Steve in prison, and Steve had given him a choice, help him and find his sister or never find her. Damien didn't even know I was Anna Cowles' daughter when we first met, I told him when he woke up the next morning. He had taken me because he had to for his sister, but he never forced himself on me or even touched me while in the house. He had become distant and angry in the time we spent in Steve's house. Damien must have realized what he was doing, and given me a chance to escape after he realized Steve didn't intend for me to get out alive.

He let me escape, even though it meant he might not find his sister. Steve hadn't been expecting to meet me, but found it a pleasant surprise that he could use to his benefit. Damien kicked into action the second he realized Steve was going to come after me. He acted against the one person who knew what happened to his sister and could help him because I meant something to him. If I didn't, he wouldn't have cared about giving me up to Steve.

"You fell in love with me," I said quietly, as

Damien placed a microwaved frozen meal in front of me.

"What?" Damien questioned, thrown off by my statement. "You're mistaken, Audrey. I don't love you. I didn't fall in love with you," he stuttered as he tried to cover up the shock in his voice and the disbelief in his eyes.

"You fell in love with me, Damien," I asserted again. The ways his pupils grew and his eyes darted, attempting to avoid looking at me, I could tell he was trying to hide it even from himself.

"You're wrong. I have no feelings for you." Damien lied, as he turned on the television behind him to drown me out.

"You've been teasing me for months and you know it."

"It's fun and I was bored," he answered curtly.

"You made love to me before you even knew who I was. You let me stay the night, and in these times that's not normal," I reminded him with a smirk on my lips. I could hear him grinding his teeth together in frustration. I had hit the nail on the head; he did fall in love with me just as Steve said.

"So? You were drunk. Maybe I was just lonely and didn't want to kick you out of the house for you to get arrested."

"If you were worried about me making it home, then why didn't you just kick me out in the morning when you first woke up?" I asked, the frustration on Damien's face growing more intense.

"Because that would be rude to do to any lady."

"But I'm not just any lady, am I, Damien?"

"No, you're not."

"I knew it!" I yelled once the words left Damien's mouth, but he stopped me so he could continue.

"You're the daughter of Anna Cowles, and the only way I will figure out what happened to my sister. You're not just any girl because you're the one that's going to make years of searching and begging that maniac for help worth it. They stopped looking for her after they found her arm. It's stupid to think an animal did it, they just didn't want to keep searching in fear of finding more bodies!"

"So you needed Steve Bennett's help, and he told you the only way you'd find out is if you helped him get my mother back."

"Oh, look who finally smartened up! Yes, that's what happened. What I didn't know is I was going to be labeled as a wanted man, and hunted down."

"What did you think would happen, Damien? No one would care about a missing girl?"

"I don't know what I thought!" he yelled back.

"I noticed," I scoffed, as I picked at the dinner he had given me.

"It's not my fault, it was you! I had no idea, you were just—"

"I was just what?"

"Too easy. You were so easy to manipulate."

"Take that back!" I gasped.

"You had an interest in me that I wasn't going to pass up, not because I loved you, but because I needed some company," Damien scowled. "Then it was a coincidence that you were just the person I needed for this plan to work out. I don't love you."

"You're lying to yourself!" I screamed as he

walked away from the table. I threw the paperback book I had been reading at Steve's house, and hit him in the head with it. When the book slapped the floor, I realized I shouldn't have done that. Damien took a ragged breath and snapped when he turned to face me again.

"Fine, you want the truth so bad? I did fall for you! Not at first, at first you were just a girl that I found attractive, but the second I was trapped in that house with you—god, it was like a house of sexual tension! I couldn't stop from acting on how I felt about you, and every day it grew, but you showed no interest. The only interest you had was escaping, and I couldn't let that happen because then I'd lose you and my sister. I let you go, because it was the right thing to do, not because I wanted to."

"I do have an interest, but I had to run because you took me. I didn't want to be there, I was fighting the feelings the entire time."

"I don't care anymore, because it's not going to work out, Audrey. Look at this! I'm a wanted man and you're the girl I kidnapped. How would that look to everyone?" Damien asked, pointing at the television behind him. The headline was 'kidnapper escapes with girl' and showed a video of Damien carrying me off with Steve behind us.

"What do we do?"

"I don't know. I really don't," Damien said sadly as he walked out of the room to leave me looking at the news feed.

We were labeled and stuck with no way out.

Chapter 15

"Damien," I whispered, as I sat next to him on the couch. It was a one-bedroom house, so he voluntarily took a blanket and some pillows and offered to sleep there while we were in the house. I had been thinking everything over for the last few hours after we argued, and I thought I had a solution to our problems.

"What?" he growled, clearly still angry with me.

"I think I have an idea on how to get out of this," I said quietly, worried about how he would take the idea. It was crazy, and I was sure that he would only get angry again.

"Let's hear it, Audrey."

"I think you should take me home," I said bluntly, making Damien groan and glare at me.

"I can't just take you home, Audrey. Don't you understand–"

"Let me finish, Damien," I said, placing my hand on his leg for a few seconds before he nodded in agreement. "I think you should take me home so my parents know what's happening. They've been through this, and they should be able to help us."

"I understand that, Audrey, but Steve will be chasing after us. It's not your parents anymore; it's us. We are what he is after, in fact, he's after you, and I'm in his way of that. He won't stop until he has you, or your mother. So why would I take you back to Wilmington where you and your mother would be in the same place?"

"Because they've escaped before. They can help us!"

"You're not thinking it through, Audrey. He doesn't want your father and me, he will kill us to get what he wants—you and your mother. He may even kill you to get to your mother! We can't go back."

"But they won't put Steve behind bars again until we tell someone you aren't a kidnapper. You'll be tracked down and then taken away. He may be let go, and then he's going to come after my mother and me anyway."

"But I am. I took you, even if you were willing. I knew what I was doing and that's exactly what it looks like. I should have realized that was his plan, but I wanted to believe that I could do something to find my sister. It's doesn't look like that will happen, so I'm going with whatever gets you out of this alive, and away from Steve."

"Fine, then we can't simply take me home, what do we do?" I asked, as a loud bang sounded overhead and sent me into Damien's chest in terror. I didn't think Steve could find us again that quickly.

"Don't worry, Audrey. It's just thunder; we won't be staying here long enough for Steve to come and get you here," he whispered to comfort

94

me, as he kissed the top of my head.

"What are we going to do, Damien?"

"I like the idea of having your parents know so they can spread it around, but I can't take you back home, sweetheart. It's too risky and there's not enough benefit to risk it."

"So then what?" I asked, lifting my head and placing it on his shoulder. I could feel my heart beating faster the longer I was with him. I had really fallen for him, harder than I had for Mark. There was no ignoring it, he may have had a hard time admitting it to me, but I knew I had fallen for him.

"I think we need to put a call out to your parents. We can't tell them where we are going, but if we can let them know you are okay, then maybe we can get rid of this kidnapper issue. I don't want to have to hide from Steve and the police."

"Then what?"

"We get Steve back in jail for setting up another kidnapping. He dies, and we can go on and live our lives."

"Our lives?" I asked curiously. I was hoping Damien would stay with me after this like my father had done for my mother. It was silly to hope for that because I knew that he wouldn't want to, but who else would want to be with me after all this was over? No one would want to answer all the questions, and they wouldn't understand.

"Yeah, you'll go on to college and I get to move back home I guess. Unless everyone there hates me now, I might not move then," Damien said, placing one hand over his face as he sighed, deeply unhappy.

"I think it will all work out."

"Then you clearly don't know Steve Bennett like I do."

"Tell me about him and what happened to your sister, maybe it can help us think of a plan."

"It's not a pleasant story, Audrey. None of them are."

"We need all the information we can get. It's time that I had the information you have. I need to know now, Damien, there's no other choice," I asserted, as he hugged me closer with one arm and looked into my eyes.

His eyes were a crystal clear blue that was stunningly gorgeous. I could read the emotions in his eyes as if it were a book, until he wanted to hide the one emotion I wanted him to have the most. He was hiding his affection for me; I knew he felt it. He said it all the time at the house. What was different now?

"Fine, we can start with Steve Bennett. He married Kelly at a young age, and they were high school sweethearts that married after college. They were happy until Kelly miscarried their baby. She became so depressed that she tried to leave Steve. Of course he wouldn't let that happen and instead stole Garrett Thomas as a young child from somewhere in New Jersey. What Steve didn't realize is that by taking Garrett, it gave Kelly something more to fight for. She didn't want the child to suffer through a life like this, and she continued to try and escape. One day Steve was so angry when he chased after her, an accident happened; she fell from a cliff while running and died on impact. He killed Kelly."

"That's a horrible way to die," I said quietly.

"It gets worse. He went after girls that looked like Kelly. He went through twelve girls until your mother was taken. She had been missing a whole year before she was recovered, and reunited with her family. She and Garrett had devised a plan to get out, when Steve made the same mistake he made with Kelly. Steve brought home a daughter, who was the actual daughter of a policeman in Charleston."

"The Sparks family, James Sparks and Jessi Sparks," I said, since Damien didn't seem to know their names.

"Exactly," he said astonished. "Well, anyway, with a young girl, the plan had to change. It didn't go exactly how they wanted it. Jessi had accidentally told Steve that Anna and Garrett were in love, and sneaking behind his back. Steve flew into a rage, and what he refers to as "the chase" started. Anna and Jessi ran from the house with only a backpack, and the warning that Garrett had given them, that the cops were in on it."

Damien looked at me before continuing to make sure I was still listening to this. "When they got to Charleston, Anna realized that Garrett had been right about the police. They were working with Steve in order to keep their families safe from him, but overlooking it when it came to others' families. The police gave up Anna's location and Steve found her. She traveled for a few more days through the same woods we're in, and eventually made it back home to Harrisonburg, where Steve was arrested by the police."

"I never knew. How do you know some of that stuff? Steve wouldn't have known what Jessi and my mom left with."

"I read your mom's book. She's a good writer, and she should continue to write stories, but I think she only wrote it to get the questions out of the way. It was a page-turner, and enjoyable to a point. It's nice to know that she and Garrett stayed together after all of that."

"My mom says if he didn't stay with her through it all no one else would have come near her," I said with a smile.

"She might be right. It would have been hard for people to be around her. It would have been hard for me to be around my sister if she had gotten back. Everyone would be stepping on eggshells, afraid to say the wrong thing," Damien said with a sullen tone.

"What happened to her?"

"I don't really know. One day she was going to go meet some friends at the mall, and never came back. You see she was a lot older than me, she was taken when she was eighteen and I was about four, but I can remember my parents searching for her for months. They died before Steve Bennett was captured and they found part of my sister's body."

"And you want the whole body, why?"

"So she can be buried with my parents in a cemetery, not somewhere in the woods. She deserves to come home and be with her family."

"Do you think Steve is just going to tell you where she is?"

"I might if he turns you over to me, Audrey," a dark voice said from behind us. I turned to see Steve Bennett, drenched from the rain, standing in the doorway with a murderous look on his face. "Or maybe he can simply join his sister in death," Steve stated with a laugh as he leapt toward us.

Chapter 16

"Move!" Damien yelled, as he shoved me out of the way just as Steve collided with him. I landed inelegantly onto the floor and could only sit and watch as Damien fought with Steve. "Audrey, get out of here!" Damien yelled, as Steve's fist collided with his face.

I started to get up as Damien and Steve took their fight to the floor. They were grappling with each other, hand-to-hand, while rolling on the floor. Steve ended up on top and landed a few blows to Damien's face until Damien hit Steve as hard as he could. Steve fell back long enough for Damien to get off the floor and land a few hits himself.

"Why are you still here?" Damien asked when he caught a glimpse of me.

Before I could answer, Steve punched Damien in the stomach. It looked as if Damien was going to hit the ground from the excruciating expression on his face. Just before he did, Damien kicked out his leg and hit Steve in the face with his boot and crashed to the ground to start another wrestling match. This time I ran out of the room. If I was distracting him in a fight, he would easily lose, and then I'd be running from Steve alone. I don't know how my mom had managed that, because the mere thought of Steve chasing me through the woods was enough to make me wish I was dead.

I ran into the kitchen and started to rummage through drawers. There were no utensils or anything I could use as a weapon anywhere. I ran to the closet as footsteps started to come down the stairs. The only thing in the closet was an umbrella.

"That's not helpful," I muttered to myself.

"My thoughts on apprentices," Steve stated from behind me.

I quickly turned around with the umbrella in my hands pointed at him. He was bloody from the fight with Damien. But where was Damien?

"They can't get a simple job of getting rid of a girl done. You aren't even supposed to be alive. I should have known you'd have your mother's charm; men are weak to it."

"Stay away from me!" I yelled.

"Feisty. We'll see how long that lasts," Steve threatened, as he ripped the umbrella out of my hands and tossed it aside.

I took a few steps back and suddenly made contact with a wall. I glanced around the room, but there was no way out. I was in a dead end room with one way out, which Steve Bennett was blocking. As he stepped closer, I had to swallow the scream that was threatening to rip through my throat. Out of instinct, I tried to run, but failed.

"You look so much like your mother. I can't wait to have you and her all to myself," He grabbed me and threw me against the wall again. The scream I had been holding in erupted from my throat as Steve's lips met mine. I struggled as his hands went to my jeans, pulling them off despite my protests, but every time I struggled he hit me. The last one went to the stomach.

I felt all the air leave my lungs as I collapsed onto the ground and curled up into a ball. Tears slowly trickled out of my eyes and I tried to regain my breath. Before I could even have a chance to recover Steve was on top of me. He moved my body so my back was on the ground and my legs were spread open.

"You will never get my mother back. My father won't let it happen," I stated weakly as I tried to fight against Steve's hold on me.

"She confessed who she was, she came out of hiding, for you. She'll trade herself to protect her daughter, and as for Garrett, he's as good as dead if I ever see him again, and he knows it."

I needed to get him off me, but he was sitting on my legs and holding me down. I couldn't move and Steve knew it. He took his time tormenting me; I watched in horror as he slid his hands under my shirt and slowly maneuvered around me.

"Just relax and enjoy," Steve said as he leaned over me. I tried not to struggle too much, in case he decided to do something worse than feel me. "You're just like your mother, which means this will be amazing all over again. She saved herself for me." At that moment I couldn't help but laugh. I was afraid, but I couldn't stop. "What's so funny?" Steve demanded. I must have hurt his ego by laughing, but I couldn't stop.

"I'm not a virgin!" I laughed, my chest heaving in laughter. "Damien and I got together before he knew who I was, and I've been with another guy for about three years!"

"You little slut!" Steve screamed. I could tell he was about to beat me out of anger when a loud clank echoed through the room. I forced my eyes open to see Damien standing over Steve with a bat. Steve had fallen off of me and Damien offered his hand to me.

"Can you move?"

"Yeah, I'm fine."

"We have to get out of here," Damien said urgently as he lifted me from the ground and then picked up my jeans. He grabbed my hand and raced out of the house before Steve could recover.

"Where are we going?" I asked as he pulled me outside and toward the car.

He opened the passenger side door, and shoved me inside. I could see the worry and fear in his eyes the whole time he walked with me and put me in the car. He didn't say anything, until he started the car.

"We are getting away from here," he said as we pulled out of the driveway. I was both relieved and exhausted, so exhausted that I fell asleep in the car and didn't wake up until Damien shook me lightly.

"Audrey, get up," he whispered.

"What's up?" I said with a yawn.

"We need to get food and there's a gas station about a mile away. Put your jeans back on," he said, as he pointed to them on the floor of the car.

I didn't say anything; I was too embarrassed. I

only nodded and started to put my pants back on. I could see that bruises had formed on my legs from Steve's assault. I lifted my shirt slightly to see the bruises on my stomach and chest; I was a mess. I pulled on my jeans just as Damien pulled into the gas station.

"I'll get gas and you get food," he said as he handed me money. "Do you think you can move that much?" he asked with a gleam of worry in his eyes.

"I can," I said as I stumbled to get out of the car. Damien was immediately at my side, even though I didn't want his help. I had to do this on my own; it was for my pride. "I'm fine." I walked away from him and into the convenience store at the gas station.

I was browsing the food aisles when I came across a payphone in the back of the store. I looked at the money Damien had given me, I had enough for one phone call only. I could only hope someone answered. I dialed my home phone number and waited. There were so many rings I thought for sure that it was going to go to the message machine, but just as I was about to hang up, my dad answered the phone.

"Hello?"

"Dad, it's Audrey," I said as tears sprang into my eyes. It was so good to hear his voice again, I never thought I'd be able to talk to him again.

"Audrey, are you okay?"

"No, I'm being chased by Steve Bennett. He's after Damien and me," I explained, as I turned back to see Damien still filling up the car.

"Who's Damien?"

"He's the one that took me. He's on the news, he's been labeled as a kidnapper."

"Because he is one, Audrey. He took you from us," my father cried, not understanding what I was trying to say.

"He was doing it to find his sister, but he's not working with Steve anymore. Damien got me out of the burning house, Steve's old house, your old house, Dad." I conveniently skipped over the part where I would have told him that I came willingly with Damien, I was sure my father didn't want to hear that part of the story.

"How do you know about that?" he asked curiously.

"Damien read mom's book, he told me, and I found your journal. I have it with me; it's in a bag that Damien gave me when he let me go."

"He let you go?" he asked in disbelief.

"Yes, just before that news story came out. I spent a night in the woods, and that's when Steve found me. Without Damien I would have been taken by Steve."

"The police are using Steve to get you back home, sweetheart," he said in a frustrated tone. "I don't like it, but I don't trust this Damien person."

"Dad, you said yourself that the police are in on it. Do you think that purge really got rid of all of his supporters? I can tell you that whatever Steve is doing, it's not to get me home. He's after mom and me. If he captures me he is going to trade me for mom. If that doesn't happen, he's just going to keep me," I said, as tears ran down my face.

"He went after you already didn't he, Audrey?" he asked. I noticed that he purposefully went around the word rape, but I ignored it.

"He tried. Damien knocked him out before he could start. We're on the run now, but I don't know the plan. We can't go back home because then Steve will have mom and me in one spot, and know where we live."

"I knew the police were still rotten," he growled. "Audrey, I don't like this. It's too risky, but please stay with Damien. If he has truly turned over, I'd rather you be with him than alone with Steve after you. If you get any hint that Damien isn't there for you, you run, and run straight home. We'll deal with Steve Bennett, do you understand?"

"Yes, Dad..."

"Don't cry. Be brave. We will figure this out. Where are you?"

"Damien gave me a map when he let me go. I'm somewhere in Virginia. I was close to Charleston, I think we're heading to Harrisonburg now," I turned to see Damien coming into the store. "Dad, I have to go."

"Please be safe, Audrey. We'll find a way out of this."

"I will, and Dad, I'm sorry about what I said."

"I know you are, sweetheart. We'll see you again. I'll try to get word out so that everyone knows this Damien fellow is a friend."

"Thank you. Bye, Dad. Tell Mom I love her."

"I will," he promised, just before I hung up the phone and walked down a random food aisle and sat down crying. Damien found me like that a few seconds later.

"Is it your wounds?" he asked quietly.

"Yes. I'm sorry. I tried."

"I know you did. Just wait here and I will get the food for us," he said as he lifted my chin and looked me in the eyes. I could see the worry and fear in his eyes, but I could also see the compassion and love he had for me. I could see conflict in his eyes before he spoke again, "I love you, Audrey."

"I love you too, Damien," I answered, shocked that he had said it. His lips lightly kissed mine for a few seconds before he pulled away

"I'll be right back. Don't move, okay?" I nodded, and he turned to get food.

I had fallen for my kidnapper, escaped a mass murderer, and now I was worried about how I was going to keep Damien after all this was over. I was one messed up person.

Chapter 17

Damien had handed me a snack bar as we walked to the car. He had to support me as I walked; I was suddenly too weak to move on my own. I was emotionally and physically exhausted; I had never had to live through anything like this before, and I didn't have time to take it all in. I devoured the snack bar before I even had time to read the label. Damien took the trash from my hand and opened the car door for me.

"Take a rest please, Audrey," he said as he buckled me in and then closed the door behind him.

When the car started moving again, I fell asleep. I was shaking as I relived the fight with Steve. If Damien hadn't come in when he did, I would have been another girl that Steve stole. I shivered at the thought as I drifted into an uneasy sleep.

I was sitting at a dining table with Damien. There was a tension in the air, Damien was staring behind me, fear in his eyes, and all of a sudden I turned to see Steve. He grabbed me and dragged me to the bedroom that I had found Damien in when we were leaving the house.

"Stop screaming!" Steve yelled over my screams.

The only answer I could produce was a scream that tore at the lining of my throat. Tears poured over my eyelashes as I tried to kick him—I somehow managed to shove him off of me, but he trapped me again. He shut the door behind him and tossed me onto the bed.

He climbed on top of me, and soon pain was searing every inch of my body while I tried ineffectively to fight him off. I heard him talk to me, trying to soothe me, but once the pain took over I couldn't hear anything over my screams. I let out a terrified scream as I sat up so quickly that my seatbelt snapped back and pushed me back into the seat. There was sweat dripping down my face and down my neck. My chest was heaving along with my ragged breath. I turned to see fear in Damien's eyes.

"I'm sorry," I huffed out as I leaned back in my chair and curled up under the blanket. I didn't know where the blanket had come from, but I could assume that Damien had given it to me.

"Is there something we need to talk about?"

"I'm finally understanding why my mom kept her past a secret."

"What do you mean?" Damien asked as he rubbed his hand up and down my back to calm me down.

"I feel like I know what she went through, and I wish I had been nicer to her growing up and when I got the news of who she was."

"You have technically. You lived in the same house she did and are running from the same man, just think of me as your Garrett," he said with a calming smile.

"Yes, and that just means I should be terrified if Steve ever catches us."

"Don't worry, I won't let him catch you. We have a few more hours before we get down to the next house. Why don't you try sleeping again?" Damien suggested, as his hand left my back, leaving a cold spot where it had once been.

"Okay," I muttered as I wrapped the blanket tighter around me. There were tears that I hadn't noticed until now running down my face. My mom's life had been so difficult, no wonder all she tried to do was protect me. Those laws, while ineffective, made people feel better, like there was hope, but the real way to prevent these problems was to educate. If I had understood my mom's time in Steve Bennett's hold, then I would have been more cooperative with the rules, instead of breaking them.

I forced my eyes shut and sent myself into another dream. This time I wasn't in the house; I didn't see Steve, and most importantly I didn't hear him. Instead I was walking through the forest, on a trail.

"Audrey, wait up!" a voice called from behind me. I turned around expecting to see my father, even Mark, but instead I turned to see Damien running toward me.

I couldn't stop myself from saying it, "I was wondering when you'd catch up." A smile formed on my lips as I wrapped my arms around him and hugged him close.

"You took off without me," he laughed.

"I did not! You were taking too long," I laughed.

"You still left without me," Damien said as he hugged me back.

"I'm sorry," I said sweetly as he leaned down to kiss my cheek.

"Don't worry about it."

"I would worry about it," a chilling voice said from behind us. We turned to see Steve standing behind us. I felt Damien's hands tighten on me. "Audrey, I need you to run. Run and don't stop running until you find some place safe."

"What about you?" I asked in a worried tone.

"I will be fine, please just run. I'll protect you," Damien said, as he lightly pushed me forward. "Now run."

I took off running as he told me to, but I made the mistake of looking back. I had turned around just in time to see Steve point a gun at Damien before the shot rang out. Damien's body fell to the ground as Steve laughed. I fell to my knees and started crying. Steve continued to laugh as he walked over to me. I suddenly felt like I was being shaken and I roughly woken up.

"Audrey, wake up please!"

"What?" I cried as I finally woke up and looked at Damien's terrified expression.

"We're here. Let's get inside," he said, but I could tell that's not what he originally planned to say.

He had been on my side of the car when I woke up; I must have been completely out if I didn't wake up the first time he tried to wake me up. Damien held his hand out for me to take and he led me to the house. I noticed it was another one story house, but there were trees surrounding us. We were isolated, and I wasn't sure if that was good or not. Damien led me into the house and pointed out a bedroom, but I walked toward the couch. I curled up in the corner of the couch and forced myself to stay awake. I didn't want to sleep again, my dreams were just confusing me even more, and now I was terrified to lose Damien.

"You've had another nightmare. Come here and I'll protect you the rest of the night," Damien said as he settled onto the couch next to me. His arms wrapped around me, and just like in my dream I felt safe.

Chapter 18

We had only been at the new home for a few days when I got sick. I skipped meals because I couldn't hold them down, I was sleeping most of the day and only getting up to rush to the bathroom before I got sick. It wasn't restful sleep because of the nightmares that I was plagued with, and most times I kept Damien up with my screams. I hadn't been able to stay asleep for more than a few hours, but would be so exhausted that I'd pass out a few minutes after waking up. I could hear Damien talking to himself sometimes when I woke up. He never leaves from my side except to go to the bathroom, because every time I wake up he's there either awake or asleep.

While I sleep and continually wake up, I hear him having a debate with himself. He isn't sure if he should take me to a hospital or not. If he takes me he is captured and sentenced to death for taking me, and if he doesn't I could get worse. I could hear the strain in his voice, he wasn't sure what to do, but he didn't want me to get worse. He just didn't understand that I didn't want him to go to jail.

"I could just drop her off and leave, but then I wouldn't know if she was okay and it would kill me," he muttered to himself as I drifted out of another round of sleep. "I could take her in and stay with her, but I know the police would take me away from her before she got better," he continued. He hadn't noticed that I had woken up again.

"Why not just let me stay here?" I asked with a hoarse voice, it was scratchy and hard to understand.

"Because you're really sick, Audrey."

"But I think I'm getting better. I'm hungry," I said as I forced myself to sit up on the couch.

"I'll get you some soup," Damien said with a weak smile.

He knew I was doing this for his benefit and that I wanted to make him feel better; he could see past my facade. I had tried before to convince him that I was fine before. I went into a sudden coughing fit and wasn't able to stop. My chest was sore afterward from the force of the coughs; it felt as if I was trying to cough up a lung. I told him I was fine to travel in the morning, but during the night I got sick. I threw up repeatedly during the night and constantly felt nauseous. So we stayed for longer than he wanted.

"Here's your soup," Damien said as he handed me a small soup to-go cup.

He had to go to town twice already because he hadn't been planning on staying here this long and I wasn't in any shape to travel. Every time he went into town it created a danger for us. Someone could spot him and call the police on him. He'd either

114

never come back, or Steve would come while he was gone and take me away. Neither was particularly a good thought while I was sick because I stayed up worried about him and myself.

I glanced at the soup in my hands and for the first time felt genuinely hungry. I drank the entire thing in one sitting and sat there with a pleasant smile on my face.

"Don't get cocky, remember the last time you did that. You threw up for an hour. I was hoping you'd take it slower this time. I'll have to cut the soup in half next time," Damien said with a comforting smile.

"Sorry," I whispered with a sullen tone.

"Don't be sorry, Audrey. I'm glad you're feeling better. I just don't want you to rush it. I'm going to take care of you, you're fine," Damien said, lightly grabbing hold of my hand and offering me a gentle smile.

"Thanks. I'll be fine to travel in a few days. I think most of the sickness is gone now."

"Don't push it, Audrey. It will just make it worse in the long run," Damien pleaded, as his fingers lightly grazed my face as he moved a piece of hair out of my face.

"I think I'll be fine, though," I pushed the topic. I couldn't hold us back much longer, Steve was still out there and he had a remarkable ability to find us, it was creepy.

"We'll see in a few days then. For now, please get some sleep and don't worry, I will be here to protect you from all those nightmares," Damien said with a smile that made my heart melt.

I could see the love in his eyes he had for me and had the overwhelming urge to tell him that I loved him and kiss him. He had told me once that he loved me, and continued to show it, but he hadn't said it since. I wondered if it was because he said it to calm me down, and I couldn't stop myself from saying it now.

"Damien?" I asked to get his attention.

"Yes, sweetheart?"

"I love you," I said quietly as I quickly fell asleep again. The last thing I saw was his stunned expression before I passed out into a blissful sleep.

My eyes snapped open to reveal a courtroom. I glanced around the room to see Steve Bennett standing up in front of the crowd. I was in the back of the courtroom, completely unnoticed and seemingly just a witness.

"On thirteen counts of kidnapping we find the defendant, guilty. On seven counts of murder we find the defendant, guilty. On one count of sexual abuse we find the defendant, guilty," a young woman said from the jurors' box before sitting back down.

"It has also been decided that the death penalty will be accepted in this case. Steve Bennett you'll be held in a maximum-security prison until your execution date can be arranged. Court is adjourned," the judge stated with a slam of her gavel as Steve was led from the room.

"I'll be back for you, Anna!" Steve called as he was pulled out.

I shook my head in disgust. This is the broadcast that had been shown on television for the last few months. They showed the case repeatedly to remind people that Steve had to be taken off the streets for good. Too bad they didn't think that when they let him out of prison to find his copycat and me.

Just as I was about to walk out of the room I saw my mother stand up with my father right next to her. They held hands as they walked out with looks of relief on their faces. The crowd had been waiting for them to move before they filed out and watch my parents leave with the torture behind them. I was about to follow them when the crowd blocked my way.

It took a long time before I found my parents again. My father was overly excited and dragging my mother out of the courthouse. They ran to a car that was parked in front of the building that I was able to slip into unnoticed.

"Where are we going Garrett?" my mother asked with a laugh.

"It's a surprise," he stated with a mischievous smile on his lips. I could now see why my mother thought we looked alike when we were plotting. My father and I had the same mischievous look in our eyes and with our smiles.

I watched my parents the entire time as the scenery flew by. The landscape and town didn't mean anything to me, but my jaw dropped when we stopped at a lake. The stars shine on the surface like a mirror and caused them to dance along the gentle lull of the lake. It took my breath away; it was how my mom described their proposal.

"This is beautiful. I love it here," I heard my mom say from behind me as I got caught up in the sights.

"I bet I can make you love it even more," My father stated confidently, but when I turned around I saw Damien on one knee with a small box in his hand.

"Audrey, from the moment I first met you I knew you were the one for me. I'd never had the confidence to pick up some stranger in the bar before, but there was something special about you. I know you didn't like me locking you in the house, but I saved your life a few times and we were able to push past it. Now I want to keep you in my life, will you marry me?" Damien asked with love filling his gaze. I wasn't able to hold it back anymore from saying it.

"Yes! Yes, I'll marry you!" I screamed as I jumped into his arms and held him tight. After a few moments he moved me slightly in order to show me the ring. The ring had one large diamond in the center then had three smaller diamonds on each side with a thin silver band.

"Here's to a happy life with the one I love," Damien said, just before he kissed me and woke me up from my dream.

I turned around to see Damien sleeping in the chair, but contorted so that he could face me while he slept. It was in that moment that I realized that we both truly cared for each other, too bad it took this mess to bring us together. It made me wonder how my parents felt. My mother had been sexually abused repeatedly, and my father had watched numerous girls go through the same fate, but they were happy together. It was as if having each other erased all the bad memories and kept the good ones.

Damien looked so peaceful while he slept, and I was suddenly taken over by an overwhelming urge to be close to him. I got off the couch, and sat with him in the chair. I curled up on his chest and felt his arms move to wrap me tightly to his chest. He didn't wake up, but he held me as if he knew who it was and didn't want me to leave.

I've never felt so cared for in this moment, but it also made me wonder that if my parents got married after they made it out of Steve's hold, what's going to happen to us if we get out of this?

Chapter 19

"Damien?" I asked, as I poked him awake.

"What? Are you okay? Is there something wrong?" he asked as he jerked awake. His eyes filled with fear as he scanned the room and then finally looked at me.

"I'm fine, don't worry. It's time to go though."

"Go where?" Damien asked, wiping the sleep from his eyes.

"We need to get on the road. We need to move before Steve finds us or someone in town calls the cops on us."

"We can't leave until you're better, Audrey. I already had this conversation with you," he groaned in frustration. I wasn't easing up on him in my demands to move. If we didn't move we'd be caught—I had a bad feeling about staying here.

"Damien, we have to. It's not safe here!"

"It's not safe here? Do you have an idea what Steve's house was like? I was supposed to leave you there and never come back. I was about to as well!" he yelled, and then paused to let the words sink in.

"You were going to leave me there?" I asked, as tears prickled at the top of my eyelashes.

"I was, but then I saw what he had planned. You were supposed to die in that fire, Audrey! I couldn't leave you there, so I took you with me and gave you a real chance at freedom. The only reason I even came back was because I can't lose you. I hoped that by letting you go you'd see you'd want me too, but I ran you straight into Steve's grasp. I couldn't stand the thought of you getting hurt, so I brought you with me. Now we're both stuck running," Damien said as he slouched back into the chair.

"Where are we right now, Damien?"

"We're near Charleston. Why?"

"We need to go south. Get on the highway and travel south, we can get away from Steve and we can fix this!" I cried as I saw how hopeless he looked.

"How? How can we fix this, Audrey? Because I can't see a way to fix this."

"My parents would know, they've done this before. Maybe they can help," I suggested. I hadn't told Damien that I talked to my father yet, but maybe telling him could help us in this case. "Please, Damien, let me try. It's either this or I keep bothering you to travel.

"You have one chance. No specifics, just tell them our problem and see what they say," Damien said in defeat as he handed me a phone from his backpack. My confusion must have shown on my face because he quickly wiped it away. "It's only for emergencies. I haven't turned it on since my parents died."

I simply nodded and turned on the phone. Damien got up and left the room, leaving me alone with a constant drone of ringing.

"Hello?"

"Mom?" I asked once her voice came over the phone.

"Audrey, your father said you called him. He says that this Damien person is the one that took you, but now he's helping you, is that true?"

"Yes, it's true. He's helping me get away from Steve. We are actually hoping to move again soon."

"Steve is there?"

"Not right now, but he's following us."

"Tell me exactly what you told your father."

"Damien and I are being chased by Steve Bennett. Damien is on the news now, as the kidnapper, but he's not working with Steve anymore. Damien got me out of Steve's old house as it was burning to the ground. Just before that news story came out Damien let me go, he gave me a chance to escape. I spent a night in the woods, and that's when Steve found me. Without Damien I would have been taken by Steve," I explained, hitting the high points on the conversation.

"The police think they are using Steve to get you back home, but they don't understand what he really is," my mother stated, more to herself though.

"Dad said that the police are in on it. Do you think that purge really got rid of all of his supporters? I can tell you that whatever Steve is doing, it's not to get me home. He's after you and me. If he captures me he is going to trade me for you. If that doesn't happen, he's just going to keep me," I said as a stray tear ran down my face.

"It's okay, Audrey, you'll get through this," my mom said as a way to let me finish my story.

"He tried to take advantage of me, like he had done to you. Damien knocked him out before he could start. We're on the run now, planning to head south away from Steve. We can't go back home because then Steve will have both of us in one spot and know where we live."

"That's fine, I understand. I'm sorry you're going through this Audrey, but you have to pay attention to what I'm going to tell you; it could mean life or death."

"Okay," I whimpered.

"You need to toughen up. You need to fight for yourself and know that Damien isn't always going to be there for you. It's okay to fall in love with him, and I'm not surprised it happened, but the hard part is to tell if those feelings are real or if you're forcing them. Trust me, I understand." I heard my dad in the background say hey in protest for my mother's remarks.

"I know these feelings are real. I tried to fight them for a while, but couldn't," I said with a small smile, not surprised she had figured out that I had developed feelings for Damien. "That's fine, but you can't let feelings get in the way, you need to focus. That's why Garrett and I split up, because we had to focus on ourselves, and we couldn't do that with the other person around because we would be too distracted worrying about the other person."

"What are you saying mom?" I asked curiously.

"Splitting up is something you may have to think

about if you want both of you to survive. Sadly, that's what it comes down to sometimes."

"I will think it over."

"Good, now worry about yourselves and get out of the area. You've got to be around my old hometown. Where are you?"

"I can't tell you any specifics, ask Dad, I told him last time." There was a pause for a few moments before my mom answered again.

"I know where you are, and I have to tell you to be careful there. It's not as safe as you think it is. Take your father's warning and beware of the cops. Sometimes they aren't there to protect you."

"I understand."

"We have to make this end, Audrey. Do whatever has to be done, and just remember sometimes to keep both of you safe, you have to split up, but you also have to stick together when it counts."

"Good bye, Mom."

"I'll see you soon, Audrey," she said, as she hung up and left me sitting on the couch alone.

"What's the plan?" Damien said as he slid next to me.

"We move out tomorrow."

"Then we'll need a plan on how to show he isn't a changed man who's helping, but still the same disgusting murderer and kidnapper we know him to be," Damien spat, as he pushed off the couch and then turned around to help me up.

"What if it doesn't work?"

"Then you and your mother could very well be in for an undesirable life."

"Then let's just get out of here and finish this off, hopefully," I said, trying to liven the mood.

"Deal, we can move in the morning. Let's get some sleep before moving tonight," he said, as he looked me over to make sure that I wasn't showing any signs of sickness. "You're sleeping in a bed tonight to make sure you rest well."

"But you sleep in the bed since I've been sick."

"Then I guess you're sleeping with me tonight, beautiful," Damien said, as he leaned in and kissed me. It was a slow sensual kiss that sent sparks and shivers up my spine. I just knew that Damien felt it too as he leaned in for another.

Chapter 20

I was awoken by an audible creak and a click as a door was shut. I stretched in the warmth of the bed that Damien and I had shared together last night. He had fully intended going to sleep with me wrapped in his arms, but I wanted more than that and with a little persuasion I got what I wanted. There was a blissful smile as I thought about rolling over and taking up the entire bed, but when I went to take over the whole bed, I ran into a muscular back. I blinked repeatedly as I recovered from the shock and confusion of finding Damien in bed with me still. I could have sworn that I heard the door close, but now I wasn't so sure.

There was another creak as I rolled out of bed. I felt fear surge through me as I quickly locked the door and then moved away just as a shadow came to the door. I fell backward onto the bed as I made out two feet and the footsteps to go along with them just outside the door. Once the knob started to turn I shook Damien from his sleep.

"Damien!" I whispered urgently.

"What?" he asked sleepily, until he heard the

doorknob snap back into place as the person let go.

"Someone's here," I said, as we both looked at the shadow pace in front of the door.

"I'd say that it's us dreaming, but that would be too optimistic," Damien said quickly, throwing me my clothes and pulling on his.

"Do you think its Steve?" I whispered as Damien moved swiftly around the room.

"I wouldn't put it past him."

"What do we do?"

"We run as planned. We escape and then move on toward another life until we can find a way to prove he doesn't have your best interest at heart, or we kill him," Damien added the last part in a softer tone, probably hoping I didn't hear him, but I did.

"How do we get out of here without being seen?" I asked, pointing to the shadow under the door.

"When I first heard about the proposition, I had the feeling Steve wouldn't let me live through this little scheme of his, I made all these houses prepared for a sudden and quickly needed escape," Damien stated, as he lifted the rug and pried open a floor board to show a ladder that led under the house.

"Where's it go?"

"Out. Here, take your bag and follow the path."

I followed the order and went down the ladder, while Damien fixed the rug above us and then slipped in after me. Once the door was sealed shut the tunnel was completely dark; I couldn't see anything.

"How do we know where to go?"

"It's a straight path, just walk," Damien

answered, as the door to the bedroom slammed open loudly. "Move quickly. It's only a matter of time before he finds the trapdoor opening."

I walked as quickly as I could down the dark tunnel, but I had no idea where I was going. I could feel Damien's hand on my back pushing me forward, so I assumed we were going the right way. The walls were cold, but not hard. They seemed pliable, easily moved, and I wasn't sure what it was made of. The whole tunnel was cold; I was shivering the entire time we traveled.

"Do you hear something?" I asked after a while. I could hear a muffled conversation, maybe a few conversations at once.

"Yeah, I'm not sure what it is."

"Should we stop?" I asked curiously.

"And go where, Audrey?" he asked sarcastically, as he pushed me foreword again.

"I was just asking," I growled, until I slammed my foot into something hard, then it turned into more of a squeal.

"Sorry, I forgot about the ladder," Damien apologized as he moved me back so he could go up first.

I couldn't see anything, but I could hear Damien's feet hitting the metal rungs of a ladder. There was a soft clank every time he moved up the ladder, but nothing else. The voices had stopped; it gave me an unsettling feeling as Damien got closer and closer to the top of the ladder.

Suddenly I was blinded by a burst of light as a panel was opened to lead us outside. I tried to look up, but all I could see was Damien's silhouette and a bright light that was impossible to stare at for too long.

"Come on, Audrey, let's get out of here," Damien called down to me.

I was about to answer him when a loud pounding reached my ears. It sounded as if it was coming from behind me and then the trap door on the other end busted open, sending the whole tunnel into the light. I grabbed hold of the ladder and made my way up quickly, although when I got up to the top I saw Damien on the ground with his hands over his head and a gun pointed at him.

"Are you Audrey Thomas?" A police officer asked me as I popped up from the hole.

"Yes sir," I said through a shaking voice.

"You're coming with us. You're going home," the officer said as two others forced Damien off the ground and pushed him roughly toward the car.

"Wait, where are you taking him?" I cried, as I pulled my arm out of the officer's hold and ran after Damien.

I caught up to Damien, shocking the officers that were holding him, and ordered them to put him down. They just rolled their eyes at each other and another officer roughly grabbed hold of me. The jagged lift caused me to let out a scream of pain, and that sent Damien into a frenzy. We were both fighting to be with the other, but the officers wouldn't let us near each other. I heard them slam Damien's head into the side of the car as they forced him in and locked the doors. Then I was put into a separate car and quickly driven off.

"What's going to happen to Damien?" I asked

through the grate in the car. I was in the back like some sort of criminal. Trapped by the bars and cage structure that made up the back of the police car; it had a negative effect on my attitude toward the officer for treating me like this and separating Damien and me.

"He's coming, just not with you. You should be happy! We got you away from the person that kidnapped you," the officer exclaimed, clearly confused by my desire to stay with Damien.

"He didn't kidnap me. He saved me from Steve Bennett!"

At my words the officer scoffed and then laughed a little. "Steve is how we found you. He did a good job leading us to you."

"He's playing you! He's tried to kill me," I yelled.

"Maybe you're the one being played," the officer said as we pulled into the Charleston police station. There was a huge throng of people, mostly officers standing there to greet me, but there was also Steve Bennett. They had played right into his trap and now I was stuck.

I could see the villainous smile trace his lips as he mouthed, "Soon, you'll be mine."

Chapter 21

"Damien! Damien!" I cried as I saw him pull up in the car behind me. The officer that had taken me to the police station held me back when Damien was roughly pulled out of the car. His head was bleeding, blood slowly dripping down his face.

"Audrey, I'm fine. We'll work this out just like your mom said," he stated as he was pushed through the crowd.

"What did he mean by that?" the officer behind me asked.

I didn't answer. I turned and glared at him, then at his name tag, Officer Moore. I pulled my arm out of his hold and followed Damien into the police station. There were cameras flashing in my eyes and reporters shoving microphones into my face the entire time until I finally made it into the station.

"Officer Rivers, can you take care of our little friend here?" Officer Moore asked once he entered the station.

I must have gotten under his skin; he was passing me off to some other officer. I could see the younger officer roll his eyes as he groaned; he must be used to undesirables from that reaction. Officer Rivers didn't even say a word; he just motioned with his hand to follow him and then led me into an office. Once the door was shut, I had a bad feeling about him.

"Well, Miss Audrey Thomas, we haven't had a kidnapping like this since your mother was taken."

"She came here?" I asked curiously, as I tried to gauge the ominous feeling.

"Yes she did. My father was the police chief here during that time, also known as Chief Rivers," he said with a smile.

"Impressive. Are you working up to that as well?" I asked, unimpressed by who his father was. He acted as if I would know his father personally, and I didn't have a clue who he was.

"I am, and to do that I have to do grunt work. Which means getting your report on what happened. Shall we start from the beginning?" he suggested as he prepared a pen to write with.

"I ran out of my family's home after discovering my mother was Anna Cowles. She and my father had never told me, and I was appalled by the news. I left the house and went out for a few hours."

"What did you do during this time?" he asked to make me continue my story.

"I got a drink at a bar, had a few too many, and Damien took me to his house for the night. I woke up in his bed, with him on the couch downstairs; everything was fine until he learned I was Anna Cowles' daughter. He offered for me to go on a trip with him to a friend's house and I accepted. I willingly went with him and he took me to Steve

Bennett's old house."

"So you were lied to in order to manipulate you to go?"

"No, I went when he offered because I didn't want to go back home," I said slowly, and eyeing his paper to make sure he was writing down what I was actually saying.

I could tell he was trying to turn everything on Damien, and now I had to be aware of that. This officer was clearly biased, but whether it was against a possible kidnapper or not, I couldn't tell.

"Did he keep you against your will at the house?" he asked, as he looked up to see my accusing expression. "And I would like to remind you it's a federal offense to lie during a police investigation, Miss Thomas."

"Yes, I was held in the house against my will."

"How did you get here today?"

"Damien helped me escape from the house when it started to burn down. Without him I'd be dead right now."

"Touching," Officer Rivers spat sarcastically.

"He gave me a jacket with a map in it and let me out of the car. I traveled in the woods for a few hours before sleeping; when I woke up, Steve was there. He threatened horrible things, like trading me for my mother or just keeping me to himself. That's when I ran away from him and found Damien again. Steve found us and said that he would never tell Damien where his sister was buried."

"Wait, what?"

"Damien's sister was one of the girls kidnapped. Only her arm was recovered when digging for the bodies, the rest of her wasn't found. Steve told Damien if he helped him get off death row to help the police find another kidnapper, then he would tell Damien where his sister was."

"Wow, you were fed a line of straight bull-shit."

"I was not!" I retorted.

"You were played!" he yelled back at me.

"He kidnapped me at first, but he let me go! He figured out Steve's plan and he got me out of the house before it burned down. Then when we on the road, he gave me a coat with a map in it and let me go. That's when Steve found me and he wasn't interested in getting me home safe. He wants my mom!"

"Then this Damien fellow came along and took you again. When he could have brought you home sooner than this," the officer stated, completely ignoring half of what I had just said.

"Damien saved my life and my mother's!"

"Steve Bennett is under twenty-four hour watch, Miss Thomas. He wasn't going to get anywhere near your mother or you after you were found."

"That's a lie. You clearly don't know what he's capable of if you believe that."

"I know the horrors of what he did, Miss Thomas—"

"But you didn't live through them," I stated knowingly as I snatched the report out of his hands.

I added in the details of Damien letting me go and saving me, and emphasizing the threats that Steve had said to me. When I was done, I signed my name in big letters and forced the paper back into his hands with an angry glare burning into his eyes.

"There's your report," I spat, as I sat back down in the chair, crossing my arms and legs to tell him that this conversation was over.

"Thanks. I'm sure your parents will be thrilled to have you back home," he said, letting his words drip with sarcasm as he walked past me.

"I know they'll be thrilled to have Steve Bennett back on death row," I scowled, and the officer slammed the door shut behind him.

I was steaming as I sat in the small office and knew that outside that door Steve Bennett was plotting for a way to get out. I got up so quickly that my chair fell backward as I stormed to the windows of the office. I could see him standing in the corner with his ever-present guard as the officer that had just interrogated me walked by him.

I watched as the officer walked up to the water fountain and simultaneously slipped the report I had just written and signed into the shredder. The sound was covered up by the noise of the water dispenser and when the shredder was done, he walked away with water spilling over the cup.

This time when he passed by Steve, there was a subtle gesture between them, nothing more than a head nod, but it was there and it told me that not all the police were on the side of justice.

Chapter 22

I was radiating such anger that it ran the risk of becoming destructive. I watched Officer Rivers as he walked around the police station and produced a piece of paper from his pocket then handed it to another officer. They nodded to each other and nothing more as they passed. Then the officer stopped and turned to look at Rivers, clearly confused.

"She didn't sign it," the other officer stated.

"Then just go ask her to," Officer Rivers said with a dismissive wave of his hand.

The new officer approached the office and caught my glare. He stopped momentarily before taking a deep breath and walking in.

"I'm sorry, I just have to have you sign the report."

"I'm not signing it until I read it," I stated forcefully.

"But you just helped him write it," he stated in a confused tone.

"I saw him shred something and I want to make sure it wasn't the real report," I said as I snatched the piece of paper out of his hands.

"That's a dangerous accusation, Audrey!"

"I don't care," I stated as I scanned the report.

"You don't understand what you're accusing!"

"I do, and I also know that I'm not the one being played. You are! Steve will run the first chance he gets!" I retorted as I continued to check the report.

All the facts were there except toward the end when he started to make it seem like Damien was keeping me from getting home and was holding me against my will. I grabbed a pen and wrote the same paragraph that I had done before then signed it and handed it to the officer. He looked a little less than pleased by my aggressive nature, but he took the paper and left. I watched him leave and head straight to a copier to make copies of my report before heading to the police chief's office on the far wall near the entrance to the station.

I watched as he walked over to a couple of other officers and repeated my warning about Steve Bennett. They laughed and a few ridiculed me, until Damien was led past them. His head was held high, but then they started to deride him instead. Two armed officers led him down a set of stairs in the far corner of the building. I left the office and skirted around the police officers in the main room as well as the other two that took Damien down stairs. The room had one large holding cell and two smaller holding cells and a desk for an officer to sit at and watch the criminals, but they were too busy celebrating upstairs to be at the post.

"Damien," I said as I approached his cell. He was lying on the cot with his hands over his eyes.

"Audrey, what are you doing down here? They said your parents had come to get you," he explained as he jumped off the cot and slipped his hands through the bars to touch my face.

"I've been stuck in an office for what feels like days. They won't tell me anything about you, and they don't believe me about Steve."

"Of course they don't believe you. They think they have him covered, but they don't. Don't worry about me by the way, I'm doing fine. In my mind I'm back in that bed with you getting ready to wake up," he said with a gentle smile, as he moved a few strands of hair away from my face.

"I wish we could've woken up like that. We would be half way to South Carolina by now," I laughed lightly, knowing that's not where he had been planning to travel.

"It just means a change of plans, Audrey. We'll get out of this and get away from Steve before he can take you. We'll just have to –"

"What are you doing down here?" Officer Rivers asked, interrupting whatever Damien had been about to say.

"I'm checking on him after police brutality," I stated sourly, pointing at the bleeding mark on Damien's forehead.

"Enough with your smart mouth. Get back to the office," he ordered as he grabbed my arm and dragged me away.

"You'll be fine, Audrey! This will all be sorted out soon," Damien called as I was forced up the stairs.

Officer Rivers very roughly and publicly shoved

me back into the office, slamming the door shut. I fell to the floor in a heap, hitting my head hard on the carpet and could hear him laughing as he walked off, but that laughter was cut short by a sudden roar of gunfire.

There were multiple shots in quick succession that barely covered the screams of the officers in the building. I was so terrified I couldn't even think about moving from my spot. I didn't know who was firing or what their goal was and right now I was probably the safest person in the building, except for Damien.

"Damien!" I said to myself. I had to help him. He was in a locked cell with no protection.

I silently berated myself for the stupidity of my actions as I made my way to the door. I opened it as silently as I could while remaining close to the floor and slowly made my way out of the office. The gunfire had ceased and there was a deadly silence in the air. There wasn't any movement from what I could see, so I made my move. I ran out of the office and down the side stairs to find Damien, but when I got there he was missing from his cell. The door was ajar and he was missing. Where could he have gone? He would have had to pass me in order to get out of here, unless he got out and hid before escaping.

"What are you doing down here?" An officer asked from behind me. He glanced between the empty cell and me before grabbing me by the arm. "Damien Clark has escaped!" He called up to the other officers.

He pushed me up the stairs and into the crowd of

police officers that were dusting off after their close call with a gunman. Some were searching the building, while others were leaving to look for Damien. I couldn't believe that Damien had left without me. I had given up my chance to escape for him, but he had left without even looking for me.

As I was forced back into the main room, the first sentence that Damien had said to me when we arrived here repeated in my mind, "We'll work this out just like your mom said." What had my mom said, and how did he know what my mom had said? I had had a private phone call with her. There were no other phones in that house, so how did he know what my mom said? He couldn't know, unless he recorded it.

I felt my eyes grow wide in realization. Damien had recorded the conversation with my mom and then tried to tell me what we had to do to escape by commenting on it. We had to part ways and escape on our own, but how was I supposed to know where to meet up with him? Where was I supposed to go?

"Where did Steve Bennett go?" An officer yelled out.

"I told you this would happen. Now you've put me and my family in danger," I growled as I glared at each of the officers that had ridiculed me for my warning.

"You have worse things to worry about. Your boyfriend has been accused of some very serious crimes and ran out without you. I'm sure Steve will find him and dispose of him before coming back for you and your mother. He has to make sure that she comes first," Officer Rivers whispered to me, but another officer overheard him and slammed him against the wall.

"You're working with Steve, just like your dad!" the officer yelled as he pulled his arm back and hit Officer Rivers in the face.

It started another police fight and gave me the chance I needed to get out of the police station. Although, the second I stepped out of the building a pair of hands grabbed me.

"Well, Audrey, it's time you came with me," Steve said, as he held his hand over my mouth and dragged me away.

Chapter 23

"Now it's time for some fun. Don't you think so, Audrey?" I tried to push off, but he wasn't letting go. I struggled against his hold as he continued to carry me off. There was just no way that he would make it out of here with all these cops around us. They would see and save me, unless they all worked with Steve. "Audrey, don't struggle," Steve growled, as we got further and further toward the back of the police station and into the woods.

I opened my mouth to scream, but couldn't with his hold on it. So I opened it as wide as I could and bit down. I heard him slam his teeth together as he tried not to let out a scream, so I bit down harder, causing him to let go of me. My right foot dug into the dirt, sending me forward in a mad sprint and trying to escape from him, but I didn't make it away fast enough. I felt hands grab my waist and pull me backwards until I slammed into his body. His hand covered my face and I got a cloth with a strong scent thrown in my face. I tried to hold my breath, but he shoved the cloth in my face and soon I felt myself start to fade.

"Enjoy your sleep, Audrey," he said deeply, as I fought to stay awake.

Fear was pulsing through my veins as he dragged my limp body toward a dark truck. There was no energy left within me to fight as the outermost parts of my vision slowly faded to black and collapsed until I blacked out completely. The last thing I remember was the slam of a car door and then I felt and heard nothing.

It took a few tries to wake up, each time I was thrown back into the darkness. I could hear the car screeching to a halt, the next time a slam, and then I wasn't even sure when I opened my eyes that I still wasn't passed out because of how dark it was. I was suddenly blinded by light before being shoved into the darkness again. The lights came repeatedly until I figured out it was streetlights and rolled over so they weren't in my eyes. I could make a faint outline of another person and saw flashes as we raced past the streetlights. I caught sight of long blonde hair and the gleam of a familiar wedding ring before I finally realized who it was.

"Mom?" I asked as I looked as the body.

I forced myself to move, but every time I moved my body screamed out in pain. I took in a sharp breath and tried to make my way over to her. Her hands were bound and she had a gag in her mouth, while I was free to move around the second I woke up. I could only imagine the fight she had put up in order to be bound and gagged in the back of the truck.

"Mom, can you hear me?" I asked, shaking her as vigorously as I could. She didn't move for a while, and it terrified me.

"Mom, get up!" I called a little louder and shook harder until she started to stretch and wake up.

"Audrey?" she asked through a cracking voice.

"Mom, you're okay."

"No, we aren't. We're in real danger, Audrey. This is exactly why we moved from here. I knew if he ever got out this would happen," she said sadly.

"I'm sorry for everything, Mom. For what I said when I left and how I reacted when I found out."

"It's understandable, but now we have to focus on how to escape before we get to that old run down house of his."

"We can't be going to the house," I said, as I started to help Mom untie the rope from her hands.

"What do you mean?"

"It caught fire when Damien and I left. That house is gone. Steve meant to destroy it and kill me inside, but Damien saved me. The house is gone and I don't know where else he would be going," I stated.

"I don't either. He had lived in that house his whole life," My mother sighed once her hands were released and her hands instantly went to her head.

"What's wrong? Are you hurt?"

"Yeah, I was injured in the struggle."

"What struggle? How were you captured?"

"Well, captured is a strong word. We had arrived at the police station to see a young man being thrown in jail for conspiracy. I wasn't surprised to find the son of Chief Rivers there, but while we were shuffling through the area to look for you because you ran off, your father and I got split up, and I was hit on the back of the head, quite swiftly and hard I might add," she said as she rubbed the back of her head.

"Is Dad okay?"

"I think so, we have to get out of here before we get wherever he plans on taking us."

"I know, but what do we do?"

"We seem to be in the bed of a pickup truck, so we can kick out the taillight and that should get rid of the holder in order to drop the tailgate. We can slide out undetected and hopefully have him continue driving for a long time," my mother said as if she had thought of the plan before.

"Wow, Mom, that's impressive."

"I tried telling you that you had to be prepared for anything," she said knowingly as she moved and let out a loud grunt as she hit out the taillight.

"Now what?" I asked curiously.

"Now you kick out the other taillight and we escape," my mom said with a smile, as if this brought her back to her childhood. I couldn't figure out why that would bring a smile to her face. Unless she was thinking about outsmarting Steve, and that made her happy.

"I can try," I stuttered, as the vehicle came to a sudden and quick stop sending us crashing into the back of the cab of the truck.

The engine shut off and a door slammed before my mother and I could recover. There was the distinguishable sound of footsteps crunching on gravel then a forceful slam of the tailgate opening.

"One of you owes me a new taillight," he said as he reached in and grabbed me by the ankles. He pulled me out and had me fall to the ground in a heap before lifting me up by my hair and directing me toward a dilapidated house. It was falling apart from years of neglect.

"Welcome home, Audrey. I think your mother and I will like it here after I fix it up a little bit."

Chapter 24

The house was one story and was falling to pieces. Even as Steve forcibly pushed me into the house I could see the damage age had done. Siding was falling off the house, while shingles were barely hanging on. I couldn't imagine having to live here and didn't want to. What was going to happen to us here? I had a strong feeling that I was going to live through a nightmare of my own.

"I have such fond memories here, Audrey," he said, as he pushed the door open and shoved me inside. My head hit the hardwood floor hard and I let out a high-pitched squeal. The sounds reverberated off the walls and all through the house as Steve continued to talk. "And now with you and Anna back in my possession, I'll have even better memories."

"Why are you doing this to us?" I cried as his hands grabbed onto a huge chunk of my hair.

"Because you're mine now, and your mother always was mine," he growled as he yanked my up by my hair. He pulled me through the house, past empty rooms with nothing in them except a chair until he found a room he liked. This room had one bed, and one seat, but nothing else. I felt a chill creep up my spine as he looked a little bit too pleased with the room he had chosen.

"This was my room whenever we came up for the summer, and now it's our family's room," he said with a smile spread across his face.

"We're not your family," I said, but just as the words left my mouth a hand landed on my cheek with a loud smack.

"Never talk to me like that! You are mine! I thought your mother would teach you better. Looks like I have to retrain her as well," Steve responded.

"You can't train people!"

"I did it before and I can do it again. You'd be amazed at what people will do if they believe they will get out alive afterward. You'll both just have to accept it for life!"

"Why can't you just take me? You said it yourself that Garrett stole Anna away from you and she was now tainted. You said I look exactly like her when you first met her. Take me and let my mother go!"

"That's quite a remarkable offer, but I need both of you. Anna is my wife, the perfect wife for me, and you are our daughter. With you here she has no reason to leave because if she does than you will be punished, and she knows exactly what it's like to be punished by me," he growled, letting the last bit of his sentence become a dark promise that he would keep if I caused trouble.

"I'm a reason to fight."

"One she won't take. You're stuck here. You

will not be leaving, and no one will come here to find you. We move in a few days, and after that, you'll lose all hope of someone coming to save you." Steve stated as he produced a pair of handcuffs.

"I have a reason to fight. I have my life to live."

"Which you will live out here now."

"Not if I have anything to say about it," I stated as I feigned bravery and reluctance to stand down.

Steve glared daggers into my eyes. I could see the anger building rapidly and knew that if I kept pushing, I would find out exactly the punishment I'd be receiving every time I misbehaved. He pulled me over to the heating vent, taking control of me by pulling my hair again. I was thrown onto the ground roughly as I heard the click of the handcuffs latch onto the heating vent—then my wrist was roughly pinched as Steve slapped on the other cuff.

"Damien will find me," I asserted, as Steve turned to walk away.

"Don't get your hopes up. He ran off without taking you with him. If he had taken you, you and my precious Anna wouldn't be here right now. I really owe it all to him, I would tell him where his sister was if I remembered. Truth is, she was one of the girls that refused to follow my rules. She was thrown out before a month was up and I didn't care about her."

"You told him that you knew where she was buried!"

"I did? Guess he didn't think I'd lie! I don't care about his sister, him, or Garrett. I only want Anna. She is meant to be with me forever! Damien was a pawn. I used him, just like I used you to get Anna. I don't care about either of you," Steve spat as he walked out of the room.

I slouched to the floor as I thought of the horrors that were about to befall my mother and me. We needed to get out, that's what I knew, but I also knew that my dad would at least be looking for us. He wouldn't stop until he found Mom and me again.

I could hear Steve's footsteps echo through the house as he re-entered the home. I tried not to look up as he came back into the room, but my mother's whimper forced me to. Steve had his hands all over her already and she was in tears. Her life was ruined if he ever laid hands on her again, and now we had to live with him again. She looked so destroyed. She thought she had been done with this man. She thought that she finally had a life. This is why she left the name Anna Cowles behind her. Now, the name would haunt her forever.

It was then that I knew how to make it out of this, dead or alive.

Chapter 25

I had to watch for days as Steve tried to reconnect with my mother. It was disgusting to watch and to hear. He constantly stroked her hair or face, kissed her, and tried to get her to talk to him. He wasn't going to give up, and I was just a pawn to keep her here, but I wasn't going to let that be true if I could help it.

"Come now, Anna. You know the rules, even your daughter knows them," Steve cooed to my mother when she turned her head away from him.

"How dare you-" Steve started to yell, but I interrupted.

"I don't know the rules. Damien changed them," I said defiantly.

Steve slowly turned to glare at me. He was clearly angry that his apprentice had changed the rules for me. I could see the veins in his head about to pop with frustration.

"I knew he wasn't good enough to follow through with my plans, but he got me what I wanted and that's all that matters." Steve said, his voice and demeanor drastically changing as he looked at my mother with lust in his eyes. "You know what, Anna, our daughter is right. She does look so much like you did when we first met," Steve said as he licked his lips. I squirmed under his gaze, but he enjoyed it the more I struggled.

"No, stop!" my mother called, as Steve went to un-cuff me.

"I bet, even though she had intercourse with Damien, she's as tight as you were. You were so much better than Kelly," he said, his voice dripping with lust as he looked at me and pushed his growing erection into my leg.

"Steve!" My mother called again, but Steve didn't hear her. He was too busy fantasizing about having sex with a young version of her again, and judging from the growing size of his hard-on, he liked what he was thinking about. "Steve, we are married. If you have intercourse with anyone it should be me," my mother said, shocking both Steve and me.

"Mom, no!" I screamed until Steve slapped his hand over my mouth.

"I'm glad you came to your senses, sweetheart," Steve said, getting off of me and going toward her.

"But I won't have it with you until she is out of the room," my mother said forcefully through tears, determined to find the strength to do this.

"I'll take our daughter out of the room, just for you," he growled lustfully, before he un-cuffed me from the heating vent and led me to another room in the house as quickly as he could.

"You can't do this!"

"I can and I will. Don't worry, your time will

come soon. You and your mother will be mine forever." He cuffed my hands together in the front and pressed my back into him for a few moments. "You look so much like your mother did." His erection pushed against my butt and his hands squeezed my breasts. When he got so hard I thought he would explode right then, he tossed me in the room without a word before he slammed the door.

I forced myself off the ground in anger and frustration. My mom was just going to let him get his way, and now he knew how to get her to cooperate. I wasn't going to let her do this; I couldn't let her do it. I tried to turn the knob on the door, but it stopped short; Steve had locked me in. I let out an angry scream as I tried to force the door open by slamming into it. I could hear my mother's screams as I tried to force the door open. I slammed into it with all I had, but then fell backward at the force. I collided with the hardwood flooring so hard that a piece popped up and I fell through the floorboards into a small concrete hole.

As I regained my bearings I realized just what this hole meant to my mother and me. We could get out during move out day tomorrow—one of us, and I knew who it would be. I could hear the bedpost suddenly stop banging on the walls and footsteps fast approaching as I forced myself out of the hole and sealed it shut. Steve opened the door with a triumphant smile on his face. He simply tossed my mother back into the room in a heap and shut the door behind him. My mom doesn't move for a while, but I can see that the handcuffs were off of her and this was what we needed.

"Mom, are you okay?"

"I've been better, but that's not the worst I've been through," she said in a weak voice.

I couldn't tell if she was breathing, but I could hear the tears and pain in her voice. I swallowed my fears, and my only hope for getting out of this alive and unscathed, but she had done this before and now it was my time.

"Mom, I need you to listen to me," I said without any emotion.

"What?" she grunted.

"I need you to get into this hole and not say a word until Steve and I leave tomorrow," I stated, opening the floorboards.

"No, you get in. He doesn't want you; he wants me. You get in that hole and hide," she stated, as she gained a second wind and got up to tell me what to do.

"No, I won't. You've been through this before, now it's my turn. You're the only one that can do something about it. He has to leave tomorrow because we're bringing too much attention to him. Just hide, then get out so we can get Dad and the cops that actually can help us and are willing to help us."

I could see the indecision on her face, so I didn't give her an option. She had just been taken advantage of, and now I was stronger than her. I took her by her hands, dragged her slowly over to the hole, and then moved her feet into the hole.

I gently slid her in, knowing she was in pain and this was the only way to save her. I was about to live through what she lived through, and I could only hope that I was strong like her and would be able to make it through it like she did.

"It's the only way we can both survive. We have to split up," I said, repeating her words back to her as I sealed her into the hiding spot.

Chapter 26

"Where is she?" I heard Steve scream as he barged into the room and saw that my mother was gone. He had come in this morning to see that she was gone and was completely flabbergasted as he ran out to look for her. He had torn apart the house from the sounds of crashing and movement that I could hear.

He clearly hadn't found her because he asked again, "Where is she?"

I didn't answer. I only looked at the open window that led down to a ledge where someone could jump down to the ground and escape. Steve followed my gaze and stormed to the window. I had made the jump previously, and left a shoe print on that ledge before pulling myself back in. I had to come back, because if we were both gone he would have torn the house apart and he would have found my mother. I wasn't going to let her live through this again. I had to keep her from living it again, even if it meant that I now had to live through the horrors of Steve Bennett. I would do it for her.

"I'm going to bring her back. Don't move," he

ordered, as he cuffed me to the arm of a nailed down chair.

He stormed out of the house with a slam of the door before I heard the rev of the truck's engine. He took off at full speed to find her and then soon I could no longer hear then engine.

"Audrey?" I heard my mom ask in a muffled voice through the floorboards.

"I'm still here. He won't be gone long because we have to leave soon. Stay quiet until we leave, then escape and find a way to a town to get help. I don't know where we will be going, but I will do everything I can to let you know."

"He's smarter than Damien was and actually doesn't want to let you go. You have to be on your toes and vigilant," she warned.

"I understand. Just please be quiet." I said, as I tried to stop the tears from falling down my face. Even if she couldn't see them, I knew she would be able to hear me crying.

"Audrey, you know what's going to happen once he comes back right?"

"I do. I've seen it before," I stated, as I remembered him once again taking advantage of my mother after Damien told me those stories. I finally understood what my mom went through and now I knew exactly what I was facing. Only it didn't prepare me for what I had to suffer through.

"What did you say?" my mother asked, as the rumble of the truck came back about twenty minutes later.

"Mom, stay quiet. No matter what," I said, as I held my head up high and tried to prepare myself for what was about to happen.

"I love you, Audrey."

"I love you too, Mom," I said as the door slammed open and closed.

Steve's footsteps thundered up the stairs and made his way toward the room he held us in. I just looked up to his face without a word. There were creases etched into his face in pure anger as he looked at me, but I didn't flinch. His green eyes burned into mine as he huffed out an angry breath and let out a loud frustrated scream.

"You let her go! She escaped because of you!"

"I've been chained this whole time," I stated matter-of-factly. His anger visibly increased, so I decided it was best not to talk anymore.

"We have to go. We can christen the new house before you know it," he said as he lifted me over his shoulder and carried me out of the house.

I couldn't and wouldn't want to move because it hurt so much. Maybe he knew that, or he wanted to get out quickly. Someone must have heard all that screaming I did, and I could only hope it was true. He tossed me into the truck and slammed the door shut. I could hear his footsteps on the gravel outside as I contorted myself to lean on the door. He got in and his hands were instantly on my back. I heard him sigh in pleasure as tears slipped down my cheeks, and he started the ignition.

"You'll love it with me. Your mom did," he assured me as we drove off.

I moved just enough so I could look up into the room I had been locked in as we drove off. I caught a glimpse of a person in the room and knew that my mother would be safe, for now. But, the real question was what was going to happen to me. I watched as Steve drove so that I could see where we were going, but we took highways and back routes for days in a row. He was careful to avoid the highways in the daytime because of the amount of police activity on them during the day. Back roads weren't watched as much and he sped as fast as he could.

He continually looked back in the rear-view mirror and stopped briefly to let other cars pass to make sure we weren't being followed. I hated when he stopped the most though. He took advantage of that time to punish me for letting my mother escape. Whether by touching me, or kissing me, Steve used the stop to his advantage, and I was wishing that he would never stop driving again. There was no option for me, I was trapped with him and had no way out.

My fear spiked as Steve came to yet another stop; this was the fifth one in two hours. It wasn't just any stop either. He had found an old motel in the area and decided to stop for the night. When we pulled in we were one of three cars in the motel's parking lot, with a lot of space between us all. I suddenly had a very bad feeling about this place, but I couldn't place it.

"Get out and don't say anything to anyone or I kill you," Steve threatened, as he motioned for me to follow him.

He roughly grabbed my hands and led me inside. I noticed that before he did, he peered through the window to make sure there were no posters of us, or anything out of the ordinary. We walked up to the counter to see a middle-aged man with balding hair. He looked shocked to see us, either because he knew who we were or because he was surprised to have people. He looked at me with the same shock, and I just shook my head lightly to try to tell him to stop. He could get injured if he wasn't careful. He needed to pretend that he didn't recognize Steve or myself, even though our faces must be plastered everywhere.

"How can I help you?" The man asked, seeming to take my hint that he didn't want to know who we were.

"We need a room to stay in for the night," Steve answered, handing the man cash without another word.

"Two rooms?" he said gesturing to me.

"Oh, no. This is my daughter. We are on our way to see her mother, right, sweetheart?" Steve lied, clearly noticing he was too old to fake being my husband.

"Right," I stated, taking an extra-long time to blink so the man would hopefully see something was wrong.

"Okay, well, here's the key," the man added, hesitantly taking another look at me. "I just need you to sign some papers. This will take some time, why don't you wait for your daddy over there," the man added, as he pointed me towards the books.

I just nodded and sat down in a chair. At first glance I couldn't see why the man had sent me over here, but then I saw it. Hidden behind the books were coloring pages and crayons. I picked up a book and turned my back to them so I could write out a message. I listed my name and my home number, along with my father's cell phone number. Then I carefully and slowly folded the paper and slipped it into the book. I didn't move right away, though; I pretended to keep reading so that Steve would buy it, except I flipped to the front again so that it didn't look strange.

"It's done now, honey. Let's rest up for the trip tomorrow," Steve said, calling me over to him.

I brought the book back with me and gave it back to the man, nodding a thank you as we walked out. He stopped me and called me back. "Excuse me, miss!" he said, once Steve was outside of the door.

"If you need help, call this number. It will come directly to me," the manager said, as he slipped me a piece of paper and the same book back to me.

I took the book he gave me and slipped him the one I had written on. Without saying another word, he took the paper and I went to follow Steve who was waiting for me.

"What did he ask you?"

"He gave me this book to read until we leave tomorrow," I lied, as he handed me a suitcase from the trunk.

"Why?"

"Just in case I got bored, I guess," I stated bluntly, forcing myself to wink at him and then beating myself on the inside for doing this to myself.

"You wouldn't get bored if you weren't a screamer," he said with a smile as we walked to our

161

assigned room.

I didn't say anything, but I was thinking. I was trying to find a way to end this. I just hoped one came soon. I waited until midnight, reading the same page of the book without really seeing the words. Steve finally got up to shower and I took my chance. I waited for the water to start running before I flipped through the book and called the number the manager had given me. It rang a few times until he picked up.

"Hello, it's the girl that came in this morning," I said in a hushed whisper.

"I understand, Miss Thomas. The police are already on their way."

"Thank you so much. I have to go before he gets out," was all I said before I hung up.

I breathed a sigh of relief, until I heard Steve speak, "Now, we can't have that can we?" he said hanging up the phone and pulling me out of the room back into the car. "We'll get to your punishment later. Once we get to the house," Steve promised as we quickly pulled out of the parking lot, leaving the manager standing there with no way to help me and the sirens closing in.

Chapter 27

Steve didn't let me forget the phone call. We had passed the sign for Ashland, Ohio just after Steve lost the cops on the back roads. I'm sure we had been on television for a while in a high-speed chase. So when we arrived, we had to stay in the house for a few days, and Steve used that time to punish me. The flashbacks were just as gruesome as the attacks themselves. I could hear the clothes being ripped from my body, my screams would echo through the empty house, Steve's pleasured noises filling my ears. I could still see flashes of Steve's face bearing over me, the enjoyment on Steve's face, but the worst part was that I could still feel everything. There was no end in sight and it seemed to go on for ages. My screams never stopped; the tears continued to fall. I wanted nothing more than to die before it could happen again.

Steve didn't even give me another room in the house. I had tried to escape so many times that he thought I enjoyed my punishment and that I was begging for his attention. I broke windows open and ran off whenever he opened the door, but now he wasn't taking the chance. I was his, and he wasn't letting me out of his sight. He took me everywhere, but made sure to change my appearance so that I wouldn't look like Audrey Thomas.

Unfortunately for him, I was getting the word out in small ways.

I couldn't do anything direct, but when people asked me my name, I said Anna, but then I would spell out Audrey in the dirt when Steve wasn't looking. There were small things, but I needed to do more. I needed to find a way out, because I was losing hope. These days had passed so slowly that I felt as if months had gone by in a short span of time. But today was my day because Steve had finally made a mistake. He went to go get gas after picking up supplies from a local hardware shop and ordered me to pick up some food since we weren't eating until later.

"Get whatever you want, just don't spend it all," Steve grunted as he threw bills and change into my hands.

I was about to walk off when he grabbed my shoulder and forced me to turn around. "And don't talk to anyone. You know what happens when you break my rules now," Steve said in a threatening tone.

I felt my body instantly shudder at the memory. The images instantly started resurfacing in my mind, and my body was ready to cave in on itself in a vain attempt to get rid of them.

"I know," I said, as I turned and walked off.

I walked nonchalantly into the gas station store as if I was just passing through. The man behind the counter didn't even look up when I entered; he was useless in helping me. I must have been in more shops and outdoors more than I was as a child over the last few weeks, but no one seemed to notice. Steve hadn't changed his appearance that much, but no one seemed to lift an eyebrow in his direction. He had only grown out his hair and a beard and gotten a fake name so that he could work at a garage under the table. It was off and I didn't like it, there was something very wrong here.

I made my way through the aisles without a problem, but I could feel Steve's gaze burning into my back. I walked out of his view toward the next aisle and made my move. There was a telephone on the far wall and I had just enough change to make a phone call. It was risky, but I was becoming desperate. I glanced around nervously as I picked up the phone and slid the change into the slot. My heart was thundering into my chest and my breathing was rapid and shallow. I punched in the number for my house as soon as the dial tone came up on the pay phone and waited.

The phone continued to ring, but no one picked up. With each ring I continued to look around; Steve could come at any minute and then I'd be done for. I was about to hang up when my dad answered the phone.

"Anna? Audrey?" he asked curiously.

"It's Audrey, Dad. I helped Mom escape, she's safe."

"I know. She called a little while ago from a police station in Clarksburg, West Virginia. Where are you?"

"I'm in Ashland–" I said, and then the line went dead before I could finish my sentence. I looked at the phone curiously and then felt a hand on the small of my back. The touch sent chills up my spine; I was in for it now.

"I guess I'm going to have to teach you another lesson. You must love getting punished if you keep up this behavior. Get the food, we are going home," Steve growled quietly in my ear so that only I would hear.

"No problem," I said, as I went back to the aisles and took my time. I picked up random food without really looking at the label, and once I ran out of aisles to saunter through to waste time, Steve took the food from me. He went to the counter and dropped it in front of the man without a word.

The man behind the counter didn't even look at me; he barely looked at Steve. He placed the items into a bag and handed them back to Steve before returning to his paper. I caught a glimpse— February 5th. It had been two months since Damien and I were arrested, and separated, which meant four months total since I had last been home. Now, I had sealed my fate with that phone call.

I was long past desperate now. I longed for Damien to magically show up and save me, or for my father to understand what I said and try to find me. It was a vain dream; now I had to live with pain and suffering. I miss Damien, I thought sadly to myself, as the car door slammed beside me and I was trapped yet again.

Chapter 28

When we first got here I tried everything, and Steve gave me a few passes because the other girls had tried them as well, but he didn't seem to understand that I wasn't going to give up. It's been more than a year now, and I was going to escape or die trying—and now I could see that the only way out was to die trying. It was either die here with him or die in my escape, but either was better than another day with him and his torture. I shivered at the memory and then cringed at the sudden pain in my back.

There was still pain from my last escape attempt, and it wasn't healing well. I had found a window on the second floor that opened above a lot of bushes and was willing to risk it. I had gotten onto the ledge and was about to jump when Steve pulled me back in and threw me onto the floor.

"How dare you try to escape? I've given you everything," he screamed, as he kicked me in the stomach, which rolled me over so he could kick me in the back.

The beating continued for a long time, and by the

time it stopped I could barely feel his blows. There was no fight left in me after that, I was broken and a shell of my former self. There was no way for me to get out and I was on my last bit of strength. Tears fell as I realized just how hopeless it was. I had been beaten every day; there was no stopping. I was bleeding constantly; Steve had become concerned and had a local doctor make sure I was okay. The doctor said I was fine, but recommended that he give me time to rest and that I shouldn't try to do any work around the house. That's when I realized that Steve had somehow become a prominent member in this town. People liked him and wanted to help him. It was sickening.

"Don't worry, Audrey. Everything will work out, it always does," Steve said one day as he left for work. He leaned down to kiss me and I didn't even move. My body didn't respond and my eyes lacked further expression than a blank stare. He didn't seem affected by it though; in fact, I think he liked it. He finally had the obedient wife that he always wanted.

I watched as he walked out of the door and stood there like a statue. My mind and soul were empty. Everything that mattered to me had been taken out of the world I lived in, and now I was trapped in hell with no way out. Even when I tried to escape when Steve was gone, he caught me. All of my attempts were useless, and there was no way to get out. I sighed heavily as I walked out of the room, with nowhere in mind as I walked around the empty house. It was two stories big and reminded me a lot of the house Damien had trapped me in the first time, but this time was different. There I still had the will to fight, and I also had someone I felt feelings for that didn't hurt me. Here was hell.

I continued to walk until I made it to the bathroom, and for no real reason I let out a loud scream. It was a mix of terrified and tortured as I looked at myself in the mirror. I stopped when I saw the dead look in my eyes; I was a lost soul with no way out. My hair was a mess, there was dried blood all over me, and suddenly, as I looked at my appearance, I was taken over by anger. Another monstrous scream left my body as I slammed my fists into the mirror. There was a loud crack as the mirror broke from the impact, but I didn't stop. I continued to pound the mirror, releasing my frustration, until I was in tears.

"There's no way out of this!" I cried as I slid onto the floor.

I felt the crunch of glass beneath me as I laid down and let sorrow fill where anger had once reigned. I felt so hopeless and lost, I couldn't handle it anymore, but what was there left to do? I felt a pinch as some of the glass shards dug into my skin at the change of position.

Glancing between the broken shards of glass, I had one last idea for escape. A final, desperate attempt to escape, but it was all I had left. I looked between my reflections in the broken glass and reached for a distant shard. I pictured my mother; I had saved her. I thought of my father; he would understand, but be broken. Then I thought of Damien; he would be destroyed.

That thought alone almost stopped me, but then I

heard Steve open the front door and call my name. Then without another thought, I stabbed the shard into my arm and let out a sharp scream. Steve's footsteps raced up the stairs, and I looked at the shard with disgust. I had to end it, I thought, as Steve burst through the door. I put the shard to my throat and he lunged for me.

"If you want to die so badly, it will be at my hands," he said, as he pulled me off the floor and away from the glass. "You'll die like all the other girls did; The Chase."

Chapter 29

I was tossed out of the house without a second thought. Steve threw a rag out with me, to stop the blood from gushing out, and that was it, nothing else; I was on my own. Did he think by throwing me out I wouldn't try to end this suffering? I would end it; after I ended him. If he was going to hunt me down, then I would make it my goal to bring him down. I just had to find a way to do that. I got up as quickly as I could and took off running in a random direction. I wasn't sure what I was going to do since my parents had only warned me of the dangers of people, but didn't take the time to tell me how to live in the woods. I could sharpen a stick, but I'd need a knife and I felt as if Steve had been shot and stabbed enough and he didn't die.

That's when I stopped dead in my tracks in the middle of some field that I had no idea where I was. I felt as if I had run for hours, but I wasn't sure. I knew I had covered a lot of ground before I sat down and took a rest. My thoughts couldn't help but go to Damien. I wondered where he was, what he had done for the last few months, but mostly I wondered why he left me. I know my mom had said splitting up was for the better, but that was before Steve took me.

I wouldn't have been able to leave Damien with Steve, so why had he done it to me? What was he doing while I was here, running for my life and trying to find a way out. I thought back to when he saved me from the house, the smoke was choking me, the flames were closing in, but he was still there for me. He was fighting for me, trying to save me, but now when I needed him he wasn't there. He had left without me and now I had to survive alone. I blinked a few times, trying to get rid of the tears in my eyes, and glanced around in the moonlight.

I must have fallen asleep, soon after that, because when I woke up the sun was up and I could hear Steve behind me. His voice traveled through the trees and sent me into a sprint. I didn't think he would actually come after me, but now that he was I didn't want to die. I just wanted to get out of this alive. I got up and sprinted through the trees and brush. There were bushes cutting into my legs, but I could hear Steve's laughter behind me so I kept running. There didn't seem to be a place to stop or a place to run to, so I had to run and stay alive for those that couldn't before.

I wasn't going to be another statistic in the Steve Bennett murders and kidnappings.

I continued running through the trees until I made it to some cliffs. I glanced down to see a lake below me, and that's when I got an idea. I turned around and held my arms up, not in surrender, but as if I was about to fly.

"You've lost!" I screamed at him as I stepped onto the edge of the cliff, ready to plunge into the lake below. "You don't have the pleasure to kill me. You've lost my mother, and I can guarantee that you won't find her ever again. You've lost, Steve, and the only thing you have left is you!"

"Not true, I still have you," he said as he lunged forward. I steadied myself as I took a step back and felt my feet go off the ledge, but as I dropped, Steve grabbed me and pulled me back.

He threw us both on the ground, with him on top of me laughing manically. "I won, Audrey! I still have you! There is no end because—"

I heard three loud shots ring out before Steve's body collapsed onto mine. There was something warm starting to seep through my clothing as the body was ripped away from mine. I looked up to see Damien in tears as he saw that I was okay. He immediately fell to the ground next to me and hugged me tightly to him. He sat me up after a while so I could see my parents, each with a gun, with triumphant smiles on their faces. They had successfully killed the man that made their lives and mine living hell.

"How did you find me?"

"When he went to prison, I got everything. Including the deed to the house here in Ohio. Which was hidden in one of his old books."

"Why did it take so long then?" I asked curiously.

"We needed to end this and get you out safely. Plus he had too many books and hiding places. We spent months combing through them all to finally get a lead," my father answered, as he leaned down and hugged me. "I'm glad you're safe, Audrey. I'm sorry it didn't seem as if we were fair to you growing up, but we did what we believed was best and now it's up to you to fix what parents believe now."

"I'll do it," I said confidently, as another shot went off. We all turned to see Damien standing above Steve's body with a smoking pistol in his hand.

"I had to make sure he was dead," he said in a sullen tone, as the blood pooled out of Steve's head and onto the ground around his cooling body.

"We'll find your sister one day, Damien," I responded, knowing that he was upset that he would never know what happened to her.

"Maybe, but I'm glad to have you back, Audrey." he said, hugging me again and kissing me in front of my parents.

"Like mother, like daughter," I heard my father say in a light tone as he kissed my mother. "Now let's go home."

***

I had to go to the hospital and have surgery to repair my injuries. I had broken a few bones, cracked ribs, and there was a case of malnutrition. It was hard to hear. I was told that it would be a long road to recovery because my body would fight the medication the entire time. I'd need a lot of time to heal, if I ever did. Damien comforted me as best as he could, and my father tried, but neither of them

174

really knew what to say or how to fix it, so they left and allowed my mother to do it for them. My mom and I had had a long talk and shared experience, and I finally understood that some secrets are better left a secret, but others had to be told.

"I never told you because I didn't want you to live through it, but I see now that it didn't work."

"I lived it through your eyes for a while. I had dreams, and I finally understand what you went through. I wish I had understood that before. It wasn't fair to blame you for the laws; it was others. They wanted to feel safe, but the laws made teens act out more. It put us more in danger than without the laws."

"It's okay, sweetheart. I'm glad you're safe and that you understand now. Maybe you can work to get rid of some of the laws, you'll see how much power you'll have in those choices after this. It's stressful, but if you want to see change, then you have to be the one to lead it in this case."

"Thanks, Mom. I know you'll be there for me. The dreams weren't so bad, it allowed me to see what it was like, but they also helped me understand how I felt about Damien," I said quietly, with a broad smile on my face.

"Do you love him?"

"Yes—I agreed to marry him, and for a moment the horrors of what Steve could do to me were gone."

"That's exactly how I felt when your father proposed to me," my mother said with a smile as she gave me a hug. "I'm sorry you had to live through this, but it's over now. We can both move on with our lives, and move past this."

"Do I have to change my name like you did?" I asked my mother as she got up to leave.

"That's up to you. I'm done changing names, there's nothing else to fear now that Steve is dead," she said with a smile.

"Wait, Mom!"

"Yes?"

"If I told you our story, would you write another book?" I asked.

"Why would I do that?" she asked curiously. "The first book was the only story I had to tell. It answered all the questions that people had, and I was never searched for again after it was published."

"Damien loved your first book, *Amber Alert*, and I think he'd love a sequel," I suggested with a smile.

A smile curled my mother's lips, "I'll have to have your father help me again, let's see if he's up for it. What would you like it to be called?"

"*Abducted*."

"I can work with that. I'm sure Damien would love a copy," my mother said with a laugh, as she walked out of the room.

For the first time ever, I finally felt like I had a relationship with my parents. I couldn't be more thankful for that. It's also what gave me the power and confidence to give a speech against the harsh laws that children were now put under. Even as I stepped to the podium, I knew that I had the courage to do it. I was the new voice of change, and I had a lot to say.

Epilogue

Six months later

"Well, at least I wasn't a part of *this* kidnapping by the infamous Steve Bennett," Jessi said with a roll of her eyes, as she sat down across the table from Damien and me. We had just finished explaining to her what happened since she had gotten out of training and would be leaving to join the FBI.

"Maybe you'll be in on the next one," Damien said lightheartedly.

"No thanks, my specialty is not with ghost hunters," Jessi scoffed, while the rest of the family laughed.

It was hard to believe that Steve Bennett was dead. It came down to one shot and that was it, he was gone forever. He had been cremated and tossed out just to make sure. Dad made sure of it, since he was still technically the only family Steve had. There were papers, legal ones to prove it, but of course that meant that Dad wanted to make sure Steve was dead.

There was no way to come back from the dead if you were just dust and ashes.

"Who knows, Jessi, there may be a few copycats," James said jokingly as he pointed at Damien.

"I wasn't a copycat," Damien retorted.

"You were just an accomplice. You're lucky that Audrey and her parents could knock down your sentence to three months. Even if they didn't press charges, the time had to be spent for kidnapping." James answered.

"I know. I'm just glad I got out early on good behavior. I couldn't have handled three full months in there," Damien shivered slightly and squeezed my hand for comfort.

"Just don't kidnap me or anyone else again, and you won't have to go back," I said as I kissed his cheek.

"I don't plan on it."

"How did the funeral for your sister go, Damien?" my mother asked, walking into the room with my father close behind.

"It was touching. I'm glad she's with our parents now. I can't thank you enough for convincing people to continue the search for more bodies."

"Her body needed to be found. Even if Jessi's specialty isn't in the supernatural, someone's was, and I could only imagine the horrors of being haunted by those that were trapped by Steve."

"It would make for some good horror stories, Anna," my father said with a smile and a kiss.

"I agree with, Mr. Thomas," Damien said. He was hoping my mom would start writing again. He loved her story and even asked her to sign a copy of her book while he was in jail for kidnapping me.

"You can call me Garrett, Damien, there's no need to be so formal," my father said, looking at my mother with a knowing smile.

"Did I miss something?" I asked curiously, looking between my parents, James, Jessi, and Damien, who all had the same knowing smile traced onto their lips.

"You did, in fact. I have a question for you," Damien said, as he got up from his chair and then got down on one knee. He pulled out a small black box and opened it to reveal a simple silver band and a small cut diamond in the center.

"Oh my, Damien."

"Don't get excited, it's a promise ring, not a wedding ring. I want you to finish school first, but I want to say that we certainly didn't meet under normal circumstances. I never expected to meet the love of my life at a bar and then kidnap her, but I'm glad I did. It's an experience that showed me plans don't always work out how we want them too, but often work out how they are supposed to. You are my everything. I can't think of a moment before I met you. I love you; I risked my life for you and would gladly do it again if it meant keeping you safe. That's what this experience has shown me, and there's no one else I would rather be with. This is to show you that I'll be here for you, waiting for you to finish school, and with you every step of the way."

"I love it, Damien!" I squealed, as I jumped from my chair and into his arms. We crashed onto the floor laughing and kissing each other.

"That scene looks quite familiar," I heard my father say, as Damien sat up and wrapped me in his arms, happily kissing my neck.

"I believe that was my reaction when you asked me that same question," my mother said, giving my father a kiss. "And your speech before the question was just as sappy," she added with a laugh.

"It wasn't sappy, it was heartfelt!" my father and Damien yelled at the same time as my mother and I continued laughing.

"Wow, the similarities are astonishing," James said, glancing between Damien and me to my mother and father. "Something tells me you two will get along famously," James said with a smile.

"I better be the maid of honor when that wedding happens," Jessi said, getting up from the table and rinsing her syrup-covered plate in the sink.

The room was filled with such a pleasant laughter that I never wanted it to end. For once I actually had Steve Bennett to thank for this. Without him, I'd still be rebelling, the laws would still be in place, and my family wouldn't get along. And, I wouldn't have Damien either. My parents and I were getting along better now because we had all lived through the experience of Steve Bennett, and I'm sure that's the only reason my parents were okay with Damien proposing to an eighteen year old. I had my loving family back and now a loving boyfriend. Things were looking up for everyone, and I couldn't wait to live my life with a fresh start.

About the Author

My name is Sara, I'm 19 years old, and I was born and raised in Alexandria, Virginia.

I have always been interested in writing, even started a book in elementary school, but it didn't get very far. It wasn't until high school that my friend, and writing partner, more or less forced me to join an amateur writing site. After some convincing from her, I plucked up the courage to post one of my stories. While it wasn't popular at first, I was shocked and overwhelmed by the support of readers on Wattpad, and they gave me the support and confidence to get where I am today. I continued to write for the next three years I was on the website, starting countless stories, some of which got surprisingly popular.

It's all thanks to those that supported me over the years, or I wouldn't have had the courage to post or submit my stories anywhere. I can't wait to start sharing more works and ideas with you guys, and I hope you enjoy the works.

Facebook:
https://www.facebook.com/profile.php?id=1000052
24038610

Twitter:
https://twitter.com/SaraNSchoen

Goodreads:
https://www.goodreads.com/author/show/9790618.
Sara_Schoen